I ♥ Band!

Crushes, Codas, and Corsages

I ♥ Band!

Crushes, Codas, and Corsages

by **Michelle Schusterman**

Grosset & Dunlap
An Imprint of Penguin Group (USA) LLC

GROSSET & DUNLAP
Published by the Penguin Group
Penguin Group (USA) LLC, 375 Hudson Street, New York, New York 10014, USA

USA | Canada | UK | Ireland | Australia | New Zealand | India | South Africa | China

penguin.com
A Penguin Random House Company

Cover illustration by Genevieve Kote.

Library of Congress Cataloging-in-Publication Data is available.

ISBN 978-0-448-45686-7   10 9 8 7 6 5 4 3 2 1

For the artists and the scientists,
especially those who are both

Chapter One

Spring break is really a teaser for summer. Just when you're getting used to all the sun and sleep, it's time to face that last little stretch of school before the *real* vacation starts.

Which was why I'd made a Summer Countdown Calendar the day before we came home from the lake. My brother, Chad, called it "the nerdiest thing Holly's ever done—and *that's* saying something." But I could only take so much relaxing. Especially when "relaxing" with my family meant lying in the sun until Chad inevitably picked me up and threw me into the freezing lake, forcing me into yet another Pool Noodle Battle Royale. (None of which I'd won, thanks to his unfair advantage of being, like, twice my size.)

He was right about my Summer Countdown Calendar being nerdy, though. Looking at it actually got me more excited about school than about summer break.

In my defense, I had a lot to look forward to. The sequel to *House of the Wicked,* my favorite movie, was coming out next weekend. The spring dance was in May, and the district science fair was the same weekend. And of course, I had plenty of band stuff coming up, too. There was the spring concert, which would be our last performance of the year. And our band director, Mr. Dante, had been talking about what a big deal the UIL competition was since school started back in the fall. It was less than a month away.

Which was why I spent the Sunday morning before school practicing. After pounding on the wall between our bedrooms for fifteen solid minutes, Chad fled the house. It was the first time he'd been awake before noon all week.

I took a break from "Labyrinthine Dances," our hardest UIL music, and glanced at the clock. My best friend, Julia Gordon, was supposed to be here any minute. Between my trip to the lake and her family spending their vacation with her grandparents in Galveston, we hadn't talked in over a week. Actually, I hadn't seen any of my friends since spring break started—another reason I couldn't wait to get back to school. I missed Julia like crazy, and Natasha and Gabby, too.

And Owen.

Stretching my arms, I studied my Summer Countdown Calendar, which was pinned on my bulletin board next to a picture I'd decided to call "Holly's

Haunted Zoo." It was a sketch of me standing in front of an exhibit filled with flying ghost-white alligators. My friend Owen Reynolds had drawn it at the zoo during our band trip to New Orleans. I'd made my mom take it to work and laminate it for me before I framed it, which for some reason she thought was really funny. But Owen was going to be a famous artist someday. He'd even won this huge art contest a few weeks ago and got to miss the last few days of school before spring break to go to an animation workshop in San Antonio. He was kind of awesome.

And if I was really honest with myself, Owen was a big part of why I couldn't wait for school tomorrow.

"You're *tan!*"

I spun around right before Julia tackled me. Laughing, I hugged her back.

"Farmer's tan, unfortunately." Pulling my sleeve up an inch, I pointed to the very distinct line where my skin went from blinding white to a shade darker than pale. "The weather was all over the place—not really hot enough for a bathing suit yet."

Julia grinned. "But at least your face is all pink and freckly. No, it's cute!" she added when I groaned.

"Yeah, no tanning for me this summer," I said. "It just makes me blotchy. So how was Galveston?"

Shrugging, Julia tossed her purse on my dresser. "Fine, I guess. Fun for the first few days, but by Wednesday I was hiding in the closet with a book just to get away from my cousins. A *ghost* book, Holly."

My mouth dropped. "Are you serious?" Julia was a total chicken when it came to any kind of horror stuff.

"Yeah, my grandma bought it for me. And I actually kind of liked it," she said, giggling at my shocked expression. "It was more funny than scary. Although still scary enough that I think you'd like it. I'll let you borrow it, if you want."

"Sure!" I glanced at my calendar. "So now that you've *finally* realized horror rocks, does that mean you'll come see the *House of the Wicked* sequel with me?"

Julia snorted. "Uh, *no*. Not for a million dollars." She paused, tilting her head. "Well, maybe for that. I could just wear a popcorn bucket on my head for two hours."

"Come on," I pleaded, flopping down on my bed. "I'll go see two sappy romantic movies with you. Two for one, Julia. And you could bring Seth—I bet he'd like *House*." Seth Anderson was Julia's boyfriend. Judging from the book of scary short stories he'd lent me a few weeks ago, I was pretty sure he'd appreciate the creepy brilliance that was *House of the Wicked*.

"No deal." Glancing at the bulletin board, Julia smiled a little. "Why do you want me to go so bad, anyway? Don't you already have a date for that? Oh, sorry—not a *date*," she added, her eyes comically wide. "A totally platonic hang. Like, your not-date to the spring dance. With the guy who drew that amazing picture of you. Which isn't *sappy* or *romantic* at all, nope, not one bit."

I laughed, although my sunburned face grew even

warmer. I'd asked Owen to the spring dance months ago, because we were friends and I knew we'd have fun. And he'd wanted to come see *House* with me because he liked the first one. We watched lots of movies together.

So it wasn't a date, and neither was the dance. Still, every time I looked at those two spots on the calendar, my stomach did a sort of nervous flip.

I gave Julia a pointed look. "Owen and I are—"

"Just friends!" Julia yelled, then collapsed on the bed next to me, giggling. "I know, I know."

"You don't believe me, though."

"I do!" She propped her feet up on the headboard. "I really do, Holly, I swear. I'm just giving you a hard time. Hey, have you heard from Natasha yet?"

"Nope." Natasha Prynne, our other best friend, had gone to Florida with her parents and a bunch of extended family. Reaching over, I grabbed my cell phone off my nightstand. "No calls. I'm pretty sure they had a late flight, though."

"Oh right." Tilting her head back, Julia grinned. "You were practicing before I got here, weren't you?" I shrugged when she pointed to my French horn sitting on my desk chair.

"Maybe."

Julia looked amused. "You're stressed about the chair test results, right? You sounded great, Holly. There's no way you'll be last chair again."

Right before the band trip, I'd completely flaked out on practicing for one of our chair tests. Mr. Dante had given us another one before spring break, and we were supposed to get the results tomorrow. Yet another reason I couldn't wait for school. With UIL coming up, it would be pretty cool to be first chair in my section.

"Thanks," I said. "I'm not worried, though—I mean, being last chair wasn't all that bad." I rolled my eyes when she clutched her chest in shock.

"I can't believe Chad put up with you playing all morning."

"He didn't," I told her. "He drove off in the Trash Mobile a few hours ago. He probably went to Leon's house or something." Nudging Julia's arm, I smiled. "Want to go raid his horror DVDs? I think you'd like *Dark Omnibus*. It's got romance and everything."

Before she could respond, I jumped to my feet and headed to the door. "There's even a kissing scene," I added. "Right before the guy gets sucked into a book possessed by demons."

I ducked into the hall just as the pillow Julia had launched at me hit the door.

Chapter Two

"*D*oesn't count."

"Does so."

Julia glared at me, twirling the combination on her locker. "Does not. I cannot *believe* I let you talk me into watching that movie."

I grinned. "Hey, I gave you fair warning. And there was plenty of romantic junk."

"Holly, for the last time . . ." Shaking her head, Julia started cramming books into her backpack. "It doesn't count as a kissing scene when the guy's eyes turn black and *bees come out of his mouth*."

"Wow, which movie's that?"

Julia and I turned, startled. Aaron Cook smiled at us as he opened his locker, which was right next to Julia's.

"*Dark Omnibus*. It's pretty good," I told him, right as Julia said, "It's *horrible*."

Aaron laughed. "Mixed reviews."

"*Horrible,*" Julia hissed again, and I giggled.

"How was your spring break?" Aaron asked.

"Pretty good," I replied. "Went to the lake with my parents and brother. Nothing too exciting. How about you?"

"It was all right." Aaron caught several folders and books as they tumbled out of his locker. "Spent a few days in Austin with my older sister and her family. And—" He stopped, a weird look on his face, and I turned around.

"Hi!" Natasha was smiling, but she looked uncomfortable, too. Slamming her locker shut, Julia spun around with a squeal and threw her arms around Natasha.

"How was your trip? What time did you get back? Did you get my message last night? We kept texting you, but I guess you were still on the plane, and then Holly made me watch this *horrible* movie, and I'm totally traumatized and—"

Laughing, I pushed her away. "Julia, get a grip!" I hugged Natasha, then glanced at Aaron, who looked pretty focused on shoving his jumble of folders back into his locker. Aaron and Natasha had been dating ever since winter break, but she'd broken up with him on the band trip to New Orleans. A nice break-up, not like a fight or anything. But still a break-up.

Aaron finally got his locker closed, then gave us all a quick smile. "See you guys in band!" he said before taking off down the hall.

"See you." I turned to see Natasha fidgeting nervously with the strap on her backpack. "Well. That was awkward."

She made a face. "Yeah. Sorry."

"I'm sure it'll get better," Julia said. "Don't you think?"

Natasha sighed. "I hope so—I mean, we're going to see each other every day in band. I hope he doesn't hate me."

"He doesn't hate you," I assured her. "I'm sure things will go back to normal soon. So how was Florida?"

"It was amazing!" Beaming, Natasha pulled out her phone and started flipping through photos. "Check it out! I took one of every roller coaster I rode."

My eyes widened as she scrolled past what looked like a creepy old hotel. "Hang on—you actually went on *that* ride?"

Natasha nodded proudly. "Yup! You'd love it."

Grabbing Natasha's phone, Julia groaned. "Oh my God, is that, like, a haunted house? What happened to the girl who was properly scared to death of all this stuff, like me?"

"It's not a haunted house—it's a drop ride," Natasha explained. "You know, where you free-fall. Although it *was* pretty creepy, too," she added as an afterthought. "The lights flicker on and off, and the elevator goes black right before it drops. You should've seen my parents' faces when I got in line. Actually, my whole family was kind of shocked."

"This is your fault." Julia poked me in the shoulder. "You dragged her onto that roller coaster in New Orleans. You created this monster."

Still scrolling through the photos, Natasha bounced on her toes. "I started making a list of amusement parks we should go to this summer," she told me, just as the bell rang.

Grinning, I picked up my backpack. "Awesome. Maybe we can find a good haunted drop ride for Julia."

"Nooo . . . ," Julia moaned. I waved as Natasha dragged her down the hall to their history class.

𝄞

When the bell rang to end third period, I bolted from the gym to the band hall so fast I probably broke my own sprinting record in PE. The chair test results were posted outside on Mr. Dante's office door.

French Horn

1. *Natasha Prynne*
2. *Holly Mead*
3. *Owen Reynolds*
4. *Brooke Dennis*

Relieved, I headed to the cubby room. Natasha and I were constantly competing for first chair. It was a friendly rivalry, though. I still had another chair test before the end of the year—I could try for first chair one more time. And besides, I wasn't exactly bummed about sitting next to Owen.

A few kids were already getting their instruments.

I waved to Victoria Rios, who already had her trumpet out. She was talking to Max Foster near the trombone section's cubbies. Just as I was closing my case, I heard a couple of familiar voices.

"I'm telling you, it's not cheating. It's just adjusting the rules a little."

"Swapping half your deck in the middle of a game is cheating, Trevor."

Shoving my case back into my cubby, I hurried to the entrance. "Owen!"

Owen's eyes lit up. "Hi, Holly!" We had a brief, weird moment of almost hugging but just standing there smiling at each other like dorks instead. Then I thought *what the heck* and hugged him anyway, which was kind of awkward since I still had my horn.

"Hi, Holly," Trevor Wells said pointedly.

"Hey, Trevor," I said before turning back to Owen. "Okay, tell me about San Antonio! How was the workshop?"

Rolling his eyes, Trevor headed for his cubby. Owen's cheeks flushed as he pulled his sketchbook out of his backpack.

"It was great! Most of the work I did was computer animation, but I've got some stuff here. And I had a lot of ideas for our science project. Maybe—"

The bell rang, cutting him off.

"Show me at lunch?" I asked, and he nodded.

"Sure!"

While Owen went to his cubby, I headed to my

seat and found Natasha sitting next to it with a rather nervous expression. Aaron sat directly behind her, talking to Liam Park. I gave Natasha a sympathetic smile as I slipped past her to my chair. Hopefully Julia was right and things would get less awkward between Natasha and Aaron soon.

"What's this?" I picked up a brochure on my chair. "Oh . . . Lake Lindon."

"I think Mr. Dante put them on everyone's chairs before the bell," Natasha said, pointing to the brochure she'd set on her music stand. Lake Lindon Band Camp was a whole week of band-geek heaven—cabins, rehearsals, a concert, all kinds of stuff. It was where Julia and Natasha had met last summer.

"Any chance your parents will let you go this year?" Natasha asked hopefully.

Sighing, I stuck the brochure in my backpack. "Last year, they said I could go the summer before high school. But I'm definitely going to ask again."

"Hiya, ladies." Gabby Flores flopped into the chair on Natasha's other side, still tightening the mouthpiece on her saxophone. "Holly, I'm really freaking out about my paper."

I nodded in agreement. Gabby and I had first-period English together, and this morning Mr. Franks had given back our first drafts for this huge research project he'd assigned in January. Everyone's papers had been covered in red marks and scribbled notes.

"Seriously, I'm going to have to rewrite the whole

thing," Gabby said. "And it's due next week? He's crazy. How'd yours look? Hi, Owen," she added.

Shrugging, I scooted my chair back a little to let Owen pass me. "He said I need more sources. There's a lot more notes, but I haven't read them all yet."

I tried to keep my voice light, but I was already kind of stressing about the rest of the semester, and my first day back wasn't even halfway over. Between the research project, the science fair, and final exams, my countdown to summer was starting to feel more like a deadline time bomb.

Something Mr. Dante didn't help one bit when, after warm-ups, he handed out a letter for our parents. *University Interscholastic League Concert and Sight-Reading Contest* was printed in bold along the top. I scanned it quickly, even though he'd talked to us about most of this earlier this semester. A bus would take us to Ridgewood High School for the contest after first period, so our parents didn't have to worry about driving. We'd perform onstage for three judges, and they'd each give us a rating. Then we'd go to another room to sight-read a piece of music, and three more judges would rate us on that. After we got our ratings, we'd go to Spins for a pizza lunch . . . and, hopefully, to celebrate.

In the back of the band hall was a long shelf lined with trophies. Those were for Sweepstakes, which meant earning a Superior rating from all six judges on stage *and* in sight-reading. Millican had a lot of them, but not for every single year—I'd already looked. I *really* wanted us to add another trophy this year.

Mr. Dante began moving through the rows, placing a sheet of music facedown on everyone's stands. Leaning to my left, I nudged Brooke Dennis.

"You guys got Sweepstakes last year, right?" I whispered. Brooke was in eighth grade and had been in advanced band last year, too.

She nodded. "Mrs. Wendell was really excited, since it was her last year. I think that was the fifth time in a row we got Sweepstakes."

My stomach twinged with nerves. Mrs. Wendell had been the band director at Millican practically forever, but she'd retired last year. I wondered if Mr. Dante was anxious about UIL, too, since it was his first year teaching here. If he was, he sure didn't show it.

"Let's talk a bit about sight-reading," Mr. Dante said cheerfully, placing a sheet of music on Liam's stand. "Yes, Gabby?"

Gabby lowered her hand. "What's the point of them judging us on music we've never even seen before? Especially since we've already been practicing the other songs so much."

"That *is* the point." Mr. Dante handed music to the percussionists. "The music we sight-read will be quite a bit easier than our other music. But it's a way for the judges to hear how good our fundamentals are—tone, rhythms, technique. I want to try it today, so there are a few rules we need to go over."

He stepped back up to the podium and started

to explain the process. After a minute, my eyes were pretty much bulging out of my head.

The judges would set a timer. Mr. Dante would have a few minutes to talk to us about the music, but he couldn't sing melodies or clap rhythms. Then the timer would go off, and he'd get a few more minutes where he *could* sing or clap rhythms, but we still couldn't.

We couldn't play at *all*, just move our fingers along while he conducted. If we accidentally played a note or something, we could actually get disqualified. And when the timer went off again, we'd just . . . perform it. The entire song, without stopping, for the first time.

The whole thing was confusing, not to mention terrifying.

I glanced around the room. Most of the seventh-graders looked as anxious as I felt, but the eighth-graders didn't. And they'd done this last year. Maybe it wasn't as scary as it sounded.

"Let's give it a shot." Mr. Dante set a timer, then opened his score. "Go ahead and turn over your music."

I flipped the page over. Well, it *did* look a little easier than our other music. I tapped my fingers on the valves while Mr. Dante talked us through it, stopping occasionally to point out difficult parts and remind us about the coda—a separate, final few measures at the bottom of the page.

When the timer went off, I glanced at Natasha. She shrugged.

"Looks easy enough," she whispered, and I nodded.

Mr. Dante raised his hands, and everyone sat up to play. At first, we sounded pretty good. We made it through almost half the page with just a few wrong notes and one misplaced cymbal crash.

Then the trumpets came in a few beats early, and their melody didn't line up with the clarinets.

Then all the saxophones except Gabby missed a key change, and she insistently squawked the right notes louder and louder.

Then literally, like, half the band missed a repeat sign while the French horn part only had rests, so all four of us lost count and didn't know when to come back in.

I was completely freaking out, my eyes darting back and forth between the music and Mr. Dante. He looked perfectly calm, cueing sections that sounded lost and gesturing for Gabby to stop honking. For a minute, we actually did start to play together again. But I only just remembered about the coda in time. I skipped down to the last line and played the last few measures, finishing just as Mr. Dante lowered his baton.

Most of the band was still going. They stopped pretty fast when they realized he wasn't conducting anymore.

"Okay, guys," Mr. Dante said, smiling around at us. Seriously, *how* was he still so calm? "Can someone tell me what it says above measure ninety-eight? Sophie?"

"'To coda,'" Sophie Wheeler replied.

"Right," Mr. Dante agreed. "So where *is* the coda? Holly?"

I squinted at my music and found the coda symbol.

"Measure one-twelve."

"Exactly." Mr. Dante nodded. "So after we take that repeat, we play through until we see 'to coda,' and then we jump down to that symbol. I'll do my best to cue you, but you have to watch out for those signs." Opening his folder, Mr. Dante pulled out another score. "Let's take out 'Labyrinthine Dances,' please."

"That's it?" Gabby blurted out. "We're not going to work on this one anymore?"

Mr. Dante smiled. "Sight-reading, Gabby. One shot. We'll be sight-reading several times a week until UIL, but it'll be a different piece every time. So tomorrow we'll address some of the problems we ran into today, and give it another try with a new song."

Natasha and I exchanged nervous glances. He was right—one shot. And if that had been our sight-reading performance at UIL, no way would we have gotten a Sweepstakes trophy.

Half an hour so wasn't long enough for lunch. With everyone catching up after spring break, plus resuming our ongoing Warlock card game, we could've used at *least* an hour. And my fried brain really needed more of a rest before facing more projects and final-exam preparation.

I sat crammed in between Owen and Natasha.

Owen, Trevor, and Max were already swapping cards over their sandwiches with several other Warlock players. On my right, Natasha was holding her phone across the table to show Seth her Disney pictures. Next to him, Julia glanced at a photo and started choking on her cookie.

"Hang on," she sputtered, grabbing the phone. "Is that—you went *bungee jumping?*"

"What?" I cried, looking up from my Warlock cards. Natasha shook her head.

"No, it wasn't really bungee jumping," she said. "More like a slingshot. You get strapped into this thing that's attached to two giant towers, and then you get pulled back and . . . catapulted."

"That's *awesome*," Seth told her, right as Julia said, "That's *insane*."

"I was kind of nervous," Natasha admitted. "But I promised myself I'd go on any ride that looked scary. And it's over really fast, too—way faster than a roller coaster." She grinned. "It was like flying. So cool. I'd definitely do it again."

I smiled. This was the happiest I'd seen Natasha since . . . well, maybe ever. At the beginning of the year we didn't like each other at all. And even after we were friends, things were weird between us because we both liked Aaron. Then she'd started dating him, and while she seemed happy, it had been more of a nervous kind of happy. Like during lunch, when she used to go sit with Aaron and his friends and I'd get the feeling she'd almost rather stay with us.

Out of habit, I glanced over at Aaron's table. He was laughing and talking to some freckled eighth-grade girl I vaguely recognized. Wait . . . were they holding hands? I squinted, but then she stood to take her tray to the trash, and I wasn't sure if I'd imagined it.

Maybe Aaron was already dating someone else. If so, I hoped Natasha wouldn't be too upset.

"Your turn, Holly."

Looking up, I realized Owen and the other Warlock players were waiting expectantly. "Oh!" I glanced from the pile of cards in the center of the table to my own deck, then tossed a chimney-gnome card down. "Hey, I still want to see what you worked on in San Antonio," I told Owen as Erin Peale used a cursed-broom card to snag my gnome. His expression brightened.

"Oh right!" Setting his cards down, Owen opened his backpack. I glanced over to make sure Julia wasn't giving me any goofy faces like she usually did around Owen, but she and Seth still were looking at Natasha's photos.

Owen opened his sketchbook. "So we started with motion sketches—drawing a character going through one motion. See?"

I burst out laughing. Twenty stick figures holding baseball bats covered the sheet in four neat rows. From left to right, I could see the progression as a ball zoomed toward the stick figure and he swung the bat and . . . missed. Which, I had to admit, happened more often than not when Owen was on the JV team. He hated baseball, but tried out just to make his parents happy.

"The workshop got me out of the last game," Owen said with a grin. "I figured this was a good tribute."

Snickering, I flipped through several more motion sketches. When I got to a page filled with waddling penguins, I stopped. "These don't look like yours."

Owen glanced down. "Oh yeah—Ginny drew some of this stuff."

"Ginny?"

"My partner," Owen explained. "They put everyone in pairs to work on the final project."

"Oh." I nodded, doing my best to look indifferent. But imagining this Ginny person drawing penguins in Owen's sketchbook was kind of irritating. When I flipped the page, all the penguins were paired up and dancing.

Make that *very* irritating.

The bell rang, and I handed Owen his sketchbook. "So you guys made an actual cartoon?"

"Yeah!" Owen gathered up his Warlock cards. "I'll show you on Thursday. If you're still coming over after school, I mean."

"Definitely." I stuffed my cards into my backpack. "I bet we're going to have lots of work to do on Alien Park."

Alien Park was our science fair project—kind of like *Jurassic Park*, but with aliens instead of dinosaurs. I wasn't wrong about the work, either. When we got to science class, Mrs. Driscoll handed back our project outlines. And just like Mr. Franks with the research papers, she'd probably gone through a whole pack of red pens.

"Revisions due next Monday," she said, and I sighed. Sometimes I wondered if our teachers forgot we actually had other classes. Mrs. Driscoll spent most of the class period going over the new unit we were starting, on organisms and their environments, but I was kind of distracted. By Ginny and her stupid dancing penguins.

"So let's talk about habitats," Mrs. Driscoll was saying. "Some animals live in rain forests, others live in deserts, and some even in live the Arctic. We're going to take a look at their physical characteristics, as well as things like shelter and food available in their habitats . . ."

Owen leaned over. "This could help with our project. Like the Mars habitat," he whispered.

I nodded, and he started taking notes. After a few minutes, I realized I hadn't heard a word Mrs. Driscoll had said. And instead of notes, I'd doodled a penguin. But it just looked like a football with a beak.

Chapter Three

By Thursday, my school stress levels had tripled. Mr. Hernandez had assigned us a new project—creating a brochure in Spanish for visitors to Millican. I had a math test coming up, an illustrated timeline to put together for history, and a PowerPoint presentation for computer lab. And all that was just for next week.

My sheet music for "Labyrinthine Dances" looked like a blur of swimming notes by the time we finished running through it during band. I rubbed my eyes as Mr. Dante flipped on the metronome.

Boop . . . boop . . . boop . . .

After a few seconds, he flipped it back off. "That's the tempo we started with at the beginning of the year," he told us. "And here's the tempo you just played at."

Boop-boop-boop-boop-boop

I blinked. Whoa. At the beginning of the year when Mr. Dante had given us this song, I thought there was no way we'd ever be able to play it well. But gradually over the year, Mr. Dante had increased the speed. And we'd just run through the whole thing up to tempo, like it was nothing.

"One step at a time," he said, smiling. "I bet you guys didn't realize just how much progress you've made this year. When you work on something consistently, every single day, sometimes the improvement seems so small you don't even notice it. But it's happening. And on that *note*," he added with a cheesy grin, and several kids groaned, "it's time for a little sight-reading."

I watched Mr. Dante hand out another new song for sight-reading practice, thinking about what he'd said. Maybe this was why he didn't seem stressed about adding another Sweepstakes trophy to our shelf. After all, UIL wasn't tomorrow—we still had plenty of time to get better at this whole sight-reading thing.

One step at a time. Probably a good way to think about the rest of the school year, I thought. It made me feel a tiny bit better about the pile of homework I was facing.

When I got to the cafeteria after band, Julia tugged my arm before we reached the table.

"Look," she whispered, pointing. I glanced over and saw Aaron and the freckly eighth-grade girl standing in line for the soda machine. No question about it this time—he had his arm around her. They definitely looked like a couple.

I winced. "Do you think Natasha knows?"

"No idea." Julia wrinkled her nose. "Should we tell her?"

"I don't know."

Natasha would probably find out pretty quickly one way or the other. But I didn't want to be the one to tell her. She'd been so happy all week, free from worries about things like boys and jealousy and dancing penguins.

But as it turned out, we didn't have to tell Natasha.

"Sophie told me Aaron has a date to the dance," she informed us, cutting up her sandwich. "Carmen Matthews." She pointed with her fork at the freckled girl, now sitting next to Aaron.

Julia and I glanced at each other.

"Sorry," I said tentatively. Natasha looked back and forth between us.

"Don't look so worried, guys!" she exclaimed. "She was always nice to me, but I kind of had the feeling she liked him. I'm not upset or anything."

"Really?" Julia asked.

"Really." Natasha popped a sandwich piece into her mouth. "I mean, it's not exactly a great feeling. But I'm okay."

"Good," I said, relieved. "Any idea who you want to go to the dance with?"

"Actually, I've kind of been thinking about going by myself," Natasha told me. "Like you and Gabby did for the winter dance."

I smiled. "That would be really cool!"

"*Very* cool." Julia glanced down when Seth plopped a book on the table before taking a seat next to her. "Oh, did you finish that? Holly wants to borrow it."

"Almost done," Seth said. "I'll finish it tonight."

"Julia's reading horror, Natasha's riding roller coasters . . ." Sighing, I shuffled my Warlock cards. "I knew one day I'd lure you guys over to the dark side."

"This book's not *that* scary," Julia insisted. "Nothing like your horrible bees-in-the-mouth movie."

For the rest of lunch, I split my attention between their conversation and the card game with Owen. But I couldn't stop thinking about how different Natasha seemed now. She really, truly didn't seem jealous at all about Aaron's new girlfriend, even though she'd only just broken up with him a few weeks ago.

So how come I couldn't stop thinking about this Ginny girl? Owen hadn't even mentioned her since Monday. And he was just my friend, anyway. I was being ridiculous.

Tossing an enchanted-teapot card on the stack, I decided Natasha had the right idea. From now on, I wouldn't waste my time feeling jealous about something that didn't even matter.

♪

It turned out my brain had a hard time getting the rest of me to figure out I wasn't jealous anymore. I'd only been in Owen's game room for ten minutes, and already I was trying to learn more about Ginny. She was in seventh grade, too. She was from Dallas. She also liked to paint. I was trying not to be too obvious about it, but it was hard not to ask Owen questions about this girl.

"So Ginny drew that, too?" I asked, smoothing out an open page in the sketchbook. Owen's dog, Worf, lay at my feet, gnawing on a bone.

Owen glanced over from his computer screen. "Yeah."

I studied the picture closely while he typed, scratching Worf behind the ears. They must have been working on setting or something because there were no dancing animals or people in this one. It was just a pencil sketch of a waterfall, surrounded by trees and tropical flowers. The water looked like it was actually moving on the page, crashing down onto the rocks with a spray of mist.

Ginny was really talented. *Well, of course she is*, I reminded myself. She'd won the same contest Owen had. Good for her.

That's what my brain said. But my hands were itching to tear that picture right out of his sketchbook.

Especially when I realized that she might have some of Owen's drawings in *her* sketchbook, too.

"So this is the . . . Holly, are you okay?"

I glanced up to see Owen staring at me. "What?"

"Your eye's kind of twitching."

"Oh . . . no, I'm fine." I pointed to the screen. "That's the cartoon?"

Owen nodded. "It's really short, but it came out pretty good."

He tapped PLAY, and we watched. The cartoon was just a few minutes long, a super-short story about a bird trying to build a little nest on a traffic light when the wind kept blowing the twigs all over the place. I'd never really thought about making cartoons before, but looking at the way the traffic lights kept changing colors while the bird darted around trying to catch the sticks, I realized how much work it must have taken.

"That's *awesome*," I said as soon as it finished. "I can't believe you actually made that. You and Ginny, I mean. How come I didn't see any of those drawings in your sketchbook?"

"They were digital." Owen tapped a silver tablet next to his keyboard. "We drew them on the computer. Mom and Steve bought me this and some software as a surprise when I got back, so I can do a lot of the stuff I learned at the workshop at home now."

I grinned. "Wow, cool!"

"Oh, and I sketched out some stuff for our project." Owen flipped to the back of the sketchbook and showed me two pages side by side, each divided into a grid of a dozen squares filled with different images. "This is a storyboard," he explained. "It's to show the order of events in a cartoon before you start drawing it. You said something about doing a commercial for Alien Park, so here's what I've got so far."

Leaning closer, I studied each image. I recognized a lot of the ideas we'd talked about—habitats and exhibits for aliens from different planets, plus theme-park rides like a slingshot UFO (Natasha would love that) and a roller coaster that looked like the rings of Saturn had gone all loopy and crooked. Grinning, I pointed to a picture of some sort of battle involving karate and light sabers and robots. "I'm guessing this has something to do with *Cyborgs versus Ninjas?*"

Owen smiled. "Yup. Movie-themed costume laser tag."

"Someone needs to make that a real thing," I said fervently, and he laughed. "All of this looks great! Are you sure it won't be too much work?"

"It's fine. I mean, you'll do most of the display-board part of the presentation, right?" he asked. "The descriptions and stuff?"

"Definitely. Not the illustrations, though. I can't draw."

Owen nodded solemnly. "Right. I remember those study cards you made for Julia's history test last semester." He grinned when I stuck my tongue out at him. (I was pretty glad I hadn't opened my science notebook yet, though. I didn't want him to see my pathetic football penguin.)

We worked on our project for almost an hour with *Dark Planet,* one of Owen's sci-fi movies, on in the background for inspiration. I sat on the floor with dozens of colored notecards spread out in neat rows in front of me, trying to find a better way to organize our presentation (something Worf didn't help by batting at the cards whenever I moved them). Owen was scribbling on the tablet with a stylus. I kept glancing up at the screen to check his progress. This whole animation thing was so cool.

And just like Natasha, Owen seemed so much happier now, compared to earlier this semester. Owen's mom and stepdad had been so excited about him playing baseball, even though he couldn't stand it. I loved that they were just as excited about his artwork, buying him that tablet and everything. Even though he'd met Ginny the Amazing Artist, I was really glad Owen had gone to that workshop.

"Oh, I love this part." Grabbing the remote, I turned up the TV volume a little and watched as a spider-like alien crawled through an air duct behind an unsuspecting astronaut. "This movie's almost horror. The good kind, where it's not gory or anything, but still really scary because you never know what's about to happen. Like *House of the Wicked*."

Owen stayed silent for a few seconds, scrawling away on the tablet. "The second one comes out this weekend, right?" he asked at last.

"Yup." I glanced at him. "You, um . . . did you still want to see it with me?"

He nodded without looking up, but his face turned a little pink. "Yes. Maybe Saturday?"

"Okay." My stomach flipped like I was on the slingshot UFO. *Not a date*, I told myself firmly, picking up a notecard and pretending to read. *We're watching a movie right now, and this isn't a date.* Granted, it was at

Owen's house after school, and we were doing homework at the same time. Going to a theater together on the weekend was a whole different thing.

Still, that didn't make it a *date*. At least, I was pretty sure.

♪

"Of course it's a date!"

Rolling her eyes, Gabby popped a handful of M&M's into her mouth before offering me the bag. I took a few, although my stomach was too knotted up for chocolate this early in the morning.

"We hang out all the time, though," I argued. "This isn't any different. It's not a date."

"If you're so sure, then why'd you ask me?"

I opened my mouth, but couldn't think of a response.

Gabby snickered. "Besides, I bet Owen thinks it's a date."

"No way." I lowered my voice when Mr. Franks walked into the classroom. "Come on, Gabby—we're going to the dance together and he knows *that's* not a date."

"Yet," Gabby said innocently, shoving the M&M's bag into her pencil case. I rolled my eyes.

Still, I was distracted all through English class. The thing that made this so confusing was I didn't even know if I *wanted* the movie to be a date or not. I loved hanging out with Owen because we had fun, and it was . . . easy. Dating was different, though. Not that I knew from personal experience. But I'd heard plenty about Julia's and Natasha's first dates, how nervous they'd been. I didn't want to be nervous around Owen. What if it *was* a date, and it totally messed up our friendship?

On the other hand, what if it didn't?

I wasn't sure which option was scarier.

I spent most of the next few class periods trying to figure out what to wear that would work for both a date and not a date. By the time I got to the band hall, I'd pretty much gone through every possible scenario for tomorrow night in my head. Almost.

"So what time's the movie start?" Trevor asked. I glanced up from my cubby in surprise.

"What?"

"Owen invited me," he explained, opening his trombone case. Owen didn't look up from his music folder, but I saw him blink several times.

"I'm pretty sure you invited yourself," he said. Trevor shrugged.

"Same difference. So what time?"

"Um . . . it starts at seven," I told him, trying not to sound too disappointed. Or relieved. Because I felt both, which was a pretty weird mix. "My mom's driving us."

"Cool." Trevor closed his case. "I can just walk to Owen's house before."

Stellar, I thought. But before I could say anything else, Gabby appeared at my side.

"And I'll come to your house first," she announced, nudging my arm. "That way your mom won't have to make an extra trip."

I stared at her, aware of Owen doing the same thing. And probably blinking his eyelids off.

"Oh great, *you're* going?" Trevor made a face. Gabby smiled sweetly at him.

"I just decided to invite myself along." Turning, she leaned closer to me and added, "Because *that's* not rude at all."

I pretended to look for something in my case. "What are you doing?" I whispered, trying not to giggle.

"I'm helping you out!" Gabby said in a low voice, her eyes wide. "Trevor was about to screw everything up, but now it's a double date. And you owe me big-time," she added. "He's so annoying."

"You know it's a horror movie, right?" Trevor told Gabby as he walked by. "The first one was pretty freaky. Ten bucks says you run out of the theater screaming before it's halfway over."

Gabby followed him out of the cubby room. "If you really wanna win that bet, just take your shoes off," she replied cheerfully, and Trevor swatted her arm with his folder.

Laughing, I glanced at Owen. "Well, tomorrow should be . . . interesting."

He smiled. "Yeah."

As we walked into the band hall together, I wondered if Owen was relieved or disappointed. Maybe he was a little bit of both, like me.

Chapter Four

There was one good thing about knowing for sure that I wasn't going on a date with Owen—it didn't take too long to pick an outfit. I only went through three or four before choosing jeans and a tank top, plus my hoodie in case the theater AC was cranked up.

After hanging the clothes over the back of my desk chair, I went downstairs to make a sandwich. Mom stood near the phone, digging through her purse, while Dad was fitting the lid on a container of lemon squares. As I opened the pantry to grab a loaf of bread, I noticed the brochure for Lake Lindon on the counter.

"Have you looked at this band-camp stuff yet?" I asked, trying to keep my voice light. Ever since I'd brought the brochure home, I'd been trying to strike that delicate balance necessary when you ask your parents for something. I didn't want to seem *too* casual about Lake Lindon because then they might think it wouldn't be that big a deal to me if I didn't get to go. But I didn't want to beg and annoy them so much they just said "no" right away—especially considering my parents pretty much never reversed their decisions once they'd made them.

"Not yet, sweetie," said Dad. "We'll take a look tonight, okay?"

"'Kay." Shutting the refrigerator, I set a package of cold cuts on the counter and eyed them suspiciously. "Hang on—why are you both all dressed up?"

Mom didn't look up. "Housewarming party for one of my coworkers."

"I thought that was later tonight!" I cried. "You said you'd drive me to the movies, Gabby's even coming over early, what am I supposed to—"

"Holly, relax," Dad interrupted. "Chad's not working tonight. We've already talked to him about taking you."

My *brother* was driving me to the movies? With *Owen?* Oh no. No no no no no *no.*

My parents must have taken my silence as acceptance, because when they finally looked up to see me gaping at them in horror, they looked surprised.

"*Chad?*" I yelled. "He can't—you—"

Mom sighed. "It'll be fine, honey. I made him promise to be on his best behavior."

I snorted so hard, it physically hurt. "Yeah, I believe that."

"It'll be fine," Mom repeated. "We'll see you tonight, okay?"

She gave me a quick kiss on the cheek, and then

they were out the door. I stared through the kitchen window as Mom's SUV backed out of the driveway, making an extra-wide turn to avoid hitting Chad's car parked along the curb.

Oh my God, Chad's car.

The Trash Mobile. I'd be taking my friends to the movies in the *Trash Mobile*.

I stood in a sort of mortified shock for a minute. Then I forced myself to focus. Okay, so I was stuck with Chad as a chauffeur. But at least I could do something about the Dumpster-like state of the limo.

Twenty minutes later, I was dragging the garden hose down the driveway when Gabby's mom drove up. I waved to her as Gabby hopped out.

"I hope you're getting paid for this," Gabby said, staring at all the cleaning supplies I'd lined up on the sidewalk.

I shook my head. "Nope, it's voluntary. Turns out my brother's taking us, and he's not allowed to drive my dad's car. And his is seriously disgusting. I can't make you guys ride in it like this."

Gabby laughed. "Gotcha. Can I help?"

"Thanks, but you'll get all dirty," I replied. She waved dismissively.

"I can just borrow something of yours, right?"

"Oh okay!" I pulled on a pair of rubber gloves. "Check the second drawer of my dresser, there are some old T-shirts in there."

By the time Gabby came back outside, I'd stuffed

one trash bag and was working on the second. Peering through the driver's window, Gabby whistled.

"Whoa, you weren't joking!"

I looked up from the backseat, where I was trying to peel off a takeout menu stuck to the seat with what looked like hardened soy sauce. "Yeah, it's rough. You really don't have to help! Just keep me company."

But Gabby was already crawling into the front passenger seat, garbage bag in hand. "Hey, can I turn on the radio?"

"Sure! Not too loud, though," I added. "I think Chad's asleep, and he doesn't know I took his keys."

Gabby snickered, flipping through radio stations. "Would he actually be mad at you for cleaning his car?"

"Probably. He's weird about his car, I guess because he paid for half." I finally scraped up the last bit of the sticky menu. "Although if he loves it so much, I don't get why he treats it like a landfill."

Having Gabby there made cleaning the Trash Mobile a lot more fun. We joked around and sang along when good songs came on the radio, and before I knew it, the inside was vacuumed, the dashboard was shiny, and the windows were smudge-free.

I glanced at the clock. "Think we can wash the outside in ten minutes? That'll give us half an hour to get ready."

"Sure!"

Just as I swung my legs outside, I heard a muffled sound, almost like a guitar strum. Sticking my hand between the driver's seat and the console, I pulled out Chad's cell phone.

"Wow, I can't believe he hasn't missed this yet." I glanced at the screen, where a text message had appeared.

Hey, babe! I'm working @ 7 tonite & tomorrow if u want to stop by. free sundae! :)

"What the . . ." I stared at the message, and Gabby peered over my shoulder.

"'*Hey, babe!*'" she read in an overly perky voice. "Looks like your brother's got a girlfriend."

Oh, ew. Just . . . *ew.*

"That. Is. Disgusting," I announced. "That's like . . . Trash Mobile–level disgusting. Who would date my brother?"

Gabby laughed. "That girl, apparently."

Wrinkling my nose, I read the name at the top of the screen. "Amy Wells. Wow, he hasn't even mentioned her to my parents! I wonder how long—"

"Amy *Wells?*" Gabby interrupted, grabbing the phone. "Holly, that's Trevor's sister!"

"*What?*" I stared at her. "Trevor has a sister? How do you know?"

"My aunt took me to the mall a few weeks ago, and we went to Maggie Moo's for ice cream," Gabby said. "Trevor came in with his dad, and there was only one chocolate-dipped cone left, so me and Trevor were arguing over who should get it. The girl behind the counter ended up giving it to me, Trevor told her off, and

I found out she's his sister." Gabby grinned, pointing at the text message. "It says *free sundae*, see? That's so her. She's awesome, by the way," she added. "She put extra M&M's on my cone and told Trevor he needed to learn how to be *chivalrous*."

This was too much for my brain to process. "*Chivalrous?*" I sputtered. "If she thinks guys should be chivalrous, what in the *world* is she doing dating Chad? He's so—I can't even—"

Laughing, Gabby pulled me out of the car. "You do realize he probably acts a lot different around her than you, right?"

"Yeah, but still . . ." Making a face, I slammed the door closed and picked up the hose. "Ew, ew, *ew*."

Gabby added soap to the buckets of water while I hosed down the car. "You know," she mused, "you can use this to your advantage."

"What do you mean?"

"Well . . ." Gabby tossed me a soapy rag, and we started scrubbing. "You said you're worried Chad's gonna give you and Owen a hard time, right?"

"Oh, he definitely will." My brother had a habit of calling any boy I knew my "boyfriend." He also had a habit of scaring them to death by pretending to be all intimidating or whatever.

Gabby raised an eyebrow. "And he's about to be in a car with his girlfriend's little brother, right?"

"Yeah . . ."

"So, if he starts to tease you, you know . . ." Gabby

winked. "Maybe you drop a little fact about him that he wouldn't want Trevor telling Amy. That'll probably keep him quiet."

I gazed at her. "That . . . is *brilliant*."

Gabby sighed. "I am, aren't I?"

"You really are." Grinning, I picked up the hose. "So Amy seems cool, huh?"

"Very," Gabby said, nodding emphatically. "I went back last weekend, and she made me the *best* chocolate-and-marshmallow milkshake. Trevor wasn't there, though."

I tried to keep a straight face. "Why, were you hoping he'd be?"

Gabby gave me such a withering look, I couldn't help but laugh. "Holly, do not *even* go there."

"Just seems like you both really like picking on each other," I said, still giggling. Gabby rolled her eyes.

"What is this, second grade?" She stepped back as I started rinsing the suds off the car. "I don't flirt with people I like by *picking* on them. I'm more mature than that."

I snorted. "If you say so."

A second later, a dirty, soapy rag smacked me in the face. I pulled it off, sputtering, and chased Gabby around the side of the house with the hose.

Chapter Five

"I can't believe you did this."

The way Chad said it was not a compliment. Buckling his seatbelt, he stared around with a furrowed brow, like he didn't remember how to drive now that the inside of his car wasn't covered in several layers of filth.

"That's the steering wheel," I said, pointing. "Just put the key in there, and—"

"Knock it off, Holly," Chad muttered, while Gabby snickered in the backseat. "I'm looking for my phone. I thought I left it in here."

"You did!" I pulled the cell phone out of my pocket and handed it to him with a bright smile. "You got a text message, by the way. Looked kind of important."

"*Babe*," Gabby added, and I pressed my lips together to keep from laughing. Chad eyed us suspiciously, then checked his texts. After a second, he tossed the phone into a cup holder. I noticed his face was just a little bit red as we pulled away from the curb.

I cleared my throat. "So how come you haven't told Mom and Dad about your girlfriend?"

"She's not my girlfriend," Chad said shortly. "We've just gone out a few times, that's all."

"Oh." I nodded. "Got it. Not your girlfriend. Just a girl you go on dates with, who calls you *babe* and gives you free ice cream."

"You're one to talk," Chad retorted. "You haven't told them about this boyfriend of yours, either."

I shook my head. "Because he's really *not* my boyfriend. And besides, Mom and Dad have met Owen tons of times. Hey, I bet Mom would *love* to go to Maggie Moo's to meet Amy tomorrow! She could tell Amy that story about when you threw a tantrum in the shoe store when you were four." I twisted in my chair to face Gabby. "He stripped naked and ran out into the mall wearing nothing but cowboy boots. He got all the way to the food court."

Gabby burst out laughing. When we slowed to stop at a red light, Chad glared at me.

"You're dead."

"Yeah?" I shrugged. "What are you gonna do?"

Flipping on the turn signal, Chad raised an eyebrow. "I *know* you like this Owen guy, even if you keep saying you don't. Does he know you framed that goofy drawing of his and hung it up in your room? 'Cause I might have to tell him."

"What drawing?" Gabby asked immediately, and I sighed.

"Owen drew a picture of me at the zoo in New Orleans." I glanced in the rearview mirror. Gabby was grinning.

"And you *framed* it?"

"Yes. Hey, it's really good," I said defensively. "You've seen his drawings."

"Mmm-hmm."

Reaching behind my seat, I pinched Gabby on the leg. "Whose side are you on, anyway?"

She giggled, swatting my hand away. "*Does* Owen know you hung it up in your room?"

"No."

"He's about to find out," Chad said as we passed the entrance into Owen's neighborhood.

I rolled my eyes. "Fine, tell him. I'm not embarrassed about appreciating good art."

"Are you embarrassed about kissing it every morning before you go to school?" Chad asked innocently, and Gabby laughed so hard she snorted.

"I do *not*!" I cried, staring at him in horror.

Chad smirked. "I didn't ask if you *did* it, I just asked if it would embarrass you if he thought you did. Obviously, the answer is yes."

Okay. This was officially war.

"You are not telling Owen that," I said firmly.

"Watch me."

"Then I'm telling Mom your girlfriend works at Maggie Moo's so we can all go visit her."

"Whatever."

We slowed to a stop in front of Owen's house, where Owen and Trevor were sitting on the front steps. Chad turned to me, squinting like he does when he gets confused.

"Hang on. How'd you know where Amy works?"

I smiled sweetly at him. "Lucky guess."

Gabby caught my eye in the rearview mirror and winked as the back door opened. Trevor slid in first, followed by Owen. In the rearview mirror, I saw his gray eyes widen in panic when Chad turned to face him.

"Owen, right?" Chad was trying so hard to sound menacing, it came off kind of cheesy. Gabby started sniggering again.

"Yes. Hi," Owen said nervously.

"And that's Trevor," I added. "Trevor, this is my brother, Chad. Chad *Mead*."

Trevor gave me a weird look. "Uh, I know your last name, Holly."

He didn't seem to recognize Chad, at all. Maybe Amy hadn't told her family about Chad, either. Not that I could blame her.

We pulled away from the curb, and Chad cleared his throat. "So, Owen. Are you—"

"Chad, you go to Ridgewood, right?" Gabby interrupted.

Chad's brow furrowed again. "Yeah."

"Maybe you know Trevor's sister!" Gabby was practically bouncing in her seat with glee. "She goes to Ridgewood, too. Right, Trevor?"

Trevor leaned away from her, looking slightly alarmed. "Um, yeah."

"Really?" I smiled at Trevor, which only seemed to confuse him more. "What's her name?"

"Amy."

Chad pressed a little too hard on the brakes, and we lurched to a halt at a stop sign. Owen and Trevor looked completely lost, probably because Chad was shooting me a death glare while Gabby pretty much cackled.

After a few seconds of stony silence, Chad stepped on the gas. "You're *so* dead," he said in a low voice, before glancing at Owen in the rearview mirror. "So you're the artist or whatever, yeah?"

Owen blinked. "Um . . . I guess so."

"He went to an animation workshop in San Antonio right before spring break," I told Chad. "He can make actual cartoons and stuff."

"You can, seriously?" Gabby grinned at Owen. "That is *so* cool!"

"Thanks." Owen looked like he wanted to crawl into a hole.

"I know *Holly* thinks it's cool," Chad said pointedly. "You know that picture you—"

"Hey, Trevor!" I swiveled around in my seat. "Did I ever tell you about the time my brother went streaking through the mall wearing nothing but cowboy boots?"

Trevor's expression of confusion quickly changed to panic. "I—no—" he sputtered. "Why would I want to know that?"

"Holly, I swear to . . ." Gripping the steering wheel, Chad made a sharp turn into the theater parking lot. When he came to a stop in front of the box office, Owen and Trevor scrambled out like the car was on fire. Gabby followed slowly, still wiping away tears of laughter.

I smiled at Chad. "Truce?"

"*Truce?*"

"You agree not to tease me and Owen when you pick us up," I said. "And I won't tell Amy's brother any more embarrassing stories about you tonight. Unless she really *isn't* your girlfriend, and you really *don't* care what she hears. Because I've got lots of good stuff. Like the time you—"

"Okay, *fine,*" Chad interrupted. "Truce."

I beamed. "Thanks! See you at nine. Try not to mess up the car too much," I added. "I bet Amy will appreciate how nice it looks now."

Rolling his eyes, Chad shoved me out the door. "Whatever. Have fun with your *boyfriend,*" he yelled right before I shut the door.

I waved at him as the clean Trash Mobile tore out of the parking lot, then turned around and saw Owen not far from the curb, watching me. Gabby and Trevor were already standing in line (and arguing about something, judging from Trevor's flailing arms).

I hurried over to Owen, torn between feeling flattered that he'd waited for me, and panic at the realization that he'd probably heard Chad call him my boyfriend.

"Sorry," I said, not sure why I was even apologizing. Owen just smiled.

"It's okay," he said. "Ready?"

"Yup!"

As we joined the others in line, I kept glancing at Owen. There was no way he hadn't heard what Chad had said. He didn't look like he minded, though.

I felt a little flutter in my chest as I realized Gabby might have been right. Maybe this was a date after all.

Chapter Six

*A*fter getting our tickets, Gabby made a beeline for the concession stand. Owen and I hung back while she and Trevor bickered over whether popcorn was better than nachos.

"Sorry we got stuck with my brother driving," I told Owen. "My parents were busy."

"It's okay," Owen said. "He seemed kind of mad at you, though."

I grinned. "Yeah, he was trying to embarrass me. But I found out he's dating Trevor's sister, so . . . you know. Blackmail."

"Oh." Owen laughed. "So that's why you told Trevor about the streaking?"

"Yup."

After getting our drinks, we followed Gabby and Trevor up the escalator. They were still arguing about something, but I secretly thought they both looked like they were having fun. Not that they'd ever admit it.

"So what was Chad trying to embarrass you with?" Owen asked.

"What?"

Owen blinked. "In the car. Didn't you say he was trying to embarrass you?"

"Oh right." *Way to go, Holly.* I chewed my popcorn several seconds longer than necessary. "It's not a big deal," I said at last. "You know that picture you gave me, the one with the alligators from the zoo? I framed it and hung it in my room. He thought I'd be embarrassed if he told you, but I'm not." I tried to keep my voice light, but the theater suddenly felt twenty degrees warmer.

"You framed it?"

"And laminated it." *But I swear I do not kiss it every morning before school.* I popped another piece of popcorn into my mouth, willing my face to cool down. "I figured I should preserve it for when you're famous," I added before glancing up. Owen was blushing furiously, too, but he looked flattered. We smiled at each other. Then the escalator reached the top and I tripped a little, sloshing soda everywhere.

Stellar.

I was still wiping soda off my hoodie when we walked into the theater. "I like sitting at the top," Gabby said, pointing with her giant box of Skittles. We climbed the stairs, but I was so distracted trying to get the stain off my sleeve that I didn't notice Owen head down the row first. Trevor started after him, but Gabby grabbed his elbow.

"Hey!" Trevor yelped. "What?"

"Ladies first," Gabby said pointedly. "Geez, Trevor. Be *chivalrous*." She gave me an expectant look, so I followed Owen. "You owe me again," Gabby whispered behind me. "Trevor probably thinks I did that because I want to sit next to him or something."

"Do you? Ow!" Giggling, I rubbed my back where she'd jabbed me with her box of candy. Although the lights were already dimming as we sat down, that didn't stop Gabby and Trevor from arguing quietly through most of the previews. But even they stopped talking for the last one: *Mutant Clowns from Planet Z*. It was a mix of sci-fi, horror, and comedy, with the vibe of a cheesy B movie but really cool special effects. I made a mental note to warn Julia and Natasha about it. They *hated* clowns—even just the poster for this movie would probably be enough to give them nightmares for a month.

When the preview finished, Owen leaned closer. "That looks *awesome*."

I nodded, trying to ignore the flutter in my chest. "We've got to see it."

It was hard to tell in the dark, but I was pretty sure his face was pink again. And when he leaned away, it was just a little bit, so our shoulders still touched.

We were still sitting like that when the movie started. But after about twenty minutes, my stomach was flipping for a very different reason. *House of the Wicked* was great, but the sequel was *amazing*.

"Best. Movie. Ever," I whispered, watching as a little girl poured sugar on the kitchen table. The sugar slowly formed an outline of a handprint with unnaturally long fingers, as if something invisible was pressing its hand on the table right next to her. (Which, of course, it probably was.)

I kept count of how many times the others jumped at the scary parts. Really good horror movies throw a scare at you when you're least expecting it, so I was always ready for the lights to go out or a character to look in a mirror and realize something was behind her. So far, Owen had jumped twice and Gabby had jumped three times. It was harder for me to tell with Trevor since I wasn't next to him, but I was pretty sure his total was five.

Not that it was a competition or anything. But if it was, I'd totally win—I hadn't jumped once yet.

I was so into the movie that it was a while before I realized me and Owen both had our arms on the armrest between us. My eyes flickered back and forth between our hands, which were just an inch apart, and the screen, where the girl watched her father slowly approach the pantry. There was no music, just this weird, low humming sort of sound.

The father touched the doorknob.

Owen's hand moved a tiny bit closer to mine.

My heart pounded in my ears. But before I could find out if Owen was about to hold my hand, the father pulled open the pantry door and was enveloped in a massive swarm of locusts.

"*Oh my God!*" screamed Gabby. Everyone jumped, including me. Not because of the locusts—I saw that coming a mile away. But because Gabby had accidentally tossed her giant Skittles box in the air, showering us with candy.

And not just us.

"*Bees! Bees!*" yelled a guy in front of Gabby, leaping to his feet and swatting frantically around his head. His two friends were standing, too, but they figured out it was just Skittles a few seconds before the bees guy. All of them turned to stare at Gabby, who'd just picked up the box.

"Sorry," she whispered, pressing her hand to her mouth to stifle a giggle. After a second, the guy on the left snorted.

"Bees!" he cried. Then we all started cracking up, including the guy who'd yelled it in the first place, and an usher had to come tell us to keep it down. The three guys sat back down, still laughing.

For the rest of the movie, any time a character started opening a door or drawer, someone would hiss "*bees!*" and send us all into another silent fit of giggles. And in the car on the way home, we probably yelled it a hundred times before Chad hollered at us to stop. It was one of those things that seemed funnier the more we did it, I guess, because we laughed harder every time.

Although a small part of me couldn't help wondering if Owen was going to hold my hand before the whole *bees* thing.

Chapter Seven

*B*y the end of the first week of April, I wished I was still at the lake for some boring relaxation. I'd turned in a revision of my research paper on Eleanor Roosevelt for English class, only to get it back covered in more corrections. The illustrated timeline I did for history class turned out to be just the first step in a huge group project on post–Civil War Reconstruction in Texas. I'd done well on my math test, but then we started a new unit on data analysis and I kept mixing up the definitions of mean, median, and mode.

I spent half the weekend working on my research paper, and the other half finishing up the descriptions for Alien Park, which Owen and I were supposed to present to Mrs. Driscoll that Friday as kind of a practice run-through for the science fair. So I didn't really feel like I'd had a weekend at all.

On Wednesday, Mr. Dante announced that our next chair test would be the week after UIL. And for the seventh-graders, it would also count as our audition for band next year. Usually our chair tests were over exercises or sections from our music, but this time he handed out actual audition pieces, kind of like all-region.

"The seventh-graders in symphonic band will be tested over the same études," Mr. Dante explained. "The sixth-graders, too. I'll have the results posted before the spring concert."

Studying the étude, I wondered how good the sixth-grade French horn players were. Brooke would be a freshman in high school next year, but Natasha, Owen, and I would all be here. If the three of us were in advanced band again, plus a really good seventh-grader or an eighth-grader from symphonic band, our section would be pretty stellar.

With UIL coming up, we were working on sight-reading every day. And despite what Mr. Dante had said about how we might not see improvement while it was happening, I couldn't help thinking we weren't getting better at all. Sometimes Mr. Dante handed out music so simple, we probably could've sight-read it in beginner band. But this time, he gave us a song that didn't look too much easier than "Labyrinthine Dances."

"The sight-reading piece last year was about this hard," Brooke said in a low voice. Owen made a face, while Natasha and I winced. "We still got Sweepstakes, though!" Brooke added reassuringly. "We were one of the only middle schools in the district who did. And we didn't play it perfectly, either—we made a few little mistakes."

I tried to smile, but knowing last year's advanced band had gotten Sweepstakes even when the sight-reading music had been especially difficult somehow made me even more nervous.

"There are rules about how difficult a sight-reading piece can be for UIL," Mr. Dante explained. Apparently he'd noticed our looks of terror. "For our level, there can only be certain keys, time signatures, rhythms—things like that. I chose this because it's pretty much the most challenging type of piece they could throw at us."

I swallowed hard. UIL was sounding scarier and scarier. In beginner band, we'd gone to a competition, but it was at a little amusement park. All the bands had gotten trophies, and there was definitely no sight-reading. But Millican was one of the only middle-school bands in the whole district who'd gotten Sweepstakes last year. It was like we had a reputation to uphold.

Mr. Dante set his timer and talked us through the music, a song called "Triumphant Fanfare." And it wasn't nearly enough instruction time for music *this* hard. The first four measures started with just French horn and trumpet, and I wasn't quite sure I understood the rhythm. The key and the time signature changed in the same measure halfway through, and the form was kind of complicated. But before I knew it, the timer went off and it was time to play.

Lifting his hands, Mr. Dante looked expectantly at

the horns and trumpets. He began conducting, and we played the fanfare introduction.

It definitely was *not* triumphant.

Out of both sections, the only two people who played with any confidence were Aaron and Victoria. Natasha and I played completely different rhythms, and I guess we each thought the other was right, because we both tried to change and it sounded all muddled. Owen and Brooke might have played it right, but their tone was kind of shaky so it was hard to tell. And the trumpet players who had the harmony parts were seriously out of tune.

Despite our bad start, when the rest of the band came in, it began to sound better. In fact, I actually started to enjoy myself. Sight-reading was almost like a game—trying to play a song perfectly the first time through. It would've been fun if I wasn't so worried about whether we'd get Sweepstakes.

But just like the first time we'd sight-read, things fell apart at the end. I saw a repeat sign coming right before the coda and couldn't remember for the life of me if we'd already repeated that section or not. I guess I wasn't the only one, because most of the brass section ended up taking the repeat again, while the woodwinds and percussion played the coda and finished. When Mr. Dante put his hands down, too, I set my horn in my lap mid-measure with a groan.

"The curse of the coda," Mr. Dante said with a sigh. "Brass, any ideas as to how you got lost?" When no one answered, he went on. "Because no one was looking up. I know it's hard not to have your eyes glued to your music when we sight-read, but you *must* look up at me at least once every four measures, especially if you're lost. I'll cue every repeat and every entrance, and I'll definitely cue the coda."

Closing the score on his podium, he gave us an encouraging smile. "Considering how difficult that piece was, I thought you all did a great job in the middle. But what were the two weakest spots?"

Natasha raised her hand. "The beginning and the end."

"That's right." Mr. Dante nodded. "Here's the thing about sight-reading. The judges don't necessarily expect it to be perfect. They'll be listening for how well you recover from mistakes. But the two spots we want to sound best are the beginning and the end, because those are the first thing they'll hear and the last thing they'll hear. So that's where we've really got to play with confidence." Smiling, he pushed his glasses up his nose. "Even if we don't feel all that confident."

Even though he was just talking about band, I decided to apply Mr. Dante's advice about confidence to the rest of my classes. I felt like I was swimming in deadlines, projects, and final-exam preparation, but maybe if I pretended I felt like I had it all under control, I could trick myself into believing it.

Same thing with my feelings about Owen, which were kind of all over the place.

After our maybe-date to the movies, a tiny part of me had been hoping the spring dance would be a real date after all. I wasn't sure how to ask Owen about it, though. Especially since Ginny the Amazing Artist called him while we were working on Alien Park at his house Thursday after school.

"She had a question about a project we're working on," Owen explained after he hung up the phone. "It's due in a few weeks."

"A project from the workshop?"

"Yeah. It was optional," he added. "Just to get more feedback on our work. I figured it'd be good practice, and Ginny wanted to do it, too."

"Oh." I smiled, probably a little too widely. "Cool!"

Owen went back to scrawling away on the tablet. But I was having a hard time concentrating on writing a description of the alien-fish habitat. I couldn't help wondering if the reason Ginny and Owen had decided to do this optional project was really because they wanted an excuse to keep in touch. Besides, wasn't Owen drowning in enough schoolwork already, like I was?

Irritated with myself, I picked up the Saturn roller coaster card. I had no reason to be jealous. Because Owen was my friend—*just* my friend—and him being friends with some girl who happened to be a talented artist was completely fine.

I figured if I kept saying it didn't bother me, eventually it wouldn't.

We were supposed to present our science fair project to Mrs. Driscoll on Friday, so I was anxious all through lunch. Not just about talking in front of the whole class, but about the project itself. Owen and I had been working on it since last semester, and I thought we might actually have a shot at winning.

"Oh, you could totally win!" Julia said when I brought it up. "You guys put *way* more work into your project than I did."

Natasha nodded in agreement. "Plus your topic's a lot cooler. Mine's just on different types of seeds." She sighed dreamily, opening a bottle of juice. "I'd so go to Alien Park if it were real. That UFO slingshot sounds amazing."

I grinned. "Thanks. It'd be pretty cool to win—the first prize is a trip to NASA in Houston. We'd meet actual astronauts."

"And watch them train," Owen added, taking a Warlock card off the stack in the middle of the table. "And see a rocket-launch simulation."

"Do you remember what the prizes for second and third place are?" I asked him.

"I think it's money," Owen replied.

Seth nodded. "Two hundred for third, three hundred for second."

Natasha choked a little on her sandwich. "Geez, I kind of wish I'd spent more time on mine now."

"I wish I had, too. Oh, Holly, I'm finished with this." Digging through his bag, Seth pulled out a book and slid it across the table to me. Julia beamed when she saw it.

"My ghost book!" she exclaimed while I examined the cover. "Tell me what you think, okay?"

"Okay!" I tucked it into my backpack, wondering if I'd even be able to read it before summer thanks to all my schoolwork. "Hey, do you have a dress for the dance yet?"

Julia shook her head, and Natasha perked up.

"Me neither!" she said just as the bell rang. "Want to go shopping together tomorrow?"

"Yes!" I stood up, suddenly much happier. I hadn't gotten to hang out with just Julia and Natasha in a few weeks. Maybe I could bring up Ginny the Amazing Artist. Even though it didn't bother me that she'd called Owen. Really.

A fresh wave of nerves hit when I walked into science. But I was kind of excited, too. Alien Park really was pretty awesome. And even though getting up to talk in front of a classroom always made me nervous at first, I usually ended up having fun.

Mrs. Driscoll had us draw slips of paper with numbers to see in what order we'd be presenting. Owen picked number three, to my relief. The sooner, the better.

Trevor and Brent McEwan went first. Their project was called "Attack of the Carrot Clones," which made me laugh. And it really was about how you could clone carrots and other vegetables. Erin Peale and Nina Rodriguez went second with a presentation on whales. They actually had an audio recording of whales singing that was pretty amazing.

But no one else had an original cartoon. Owen hadn't finished the commercial yet, but he'd created enough images that we had a few super-short animated sequences to show with our presentation. So I felt pretty confident when it was our turn.

While Mrs. Driscoll finished giving Erin and Nina her notes, Owen fixed the computer monitor so that it faced the class and got the cartoons ready. I set up our display board with all the pictures and descriptions, then waited until Mrs. Driscoll gestured for me to start.

"Our project is called Alien Park," I told the class. "It's a theme park with rides, but also exhibits and habitats like a zoo. Only instead of animals, we have different types of aliens from planets with a variety of . . ." I glanced at my notes, clearing my throat. "A variety of ecological and environmental conditions."

I launched into the first description of amphibious aliens from Europa, one of Jupiter's moons. Owen played a short cartoon that showed them swimming around in their habitat, followed by another one of our Saturn roller coaster.

"Awesome!" said Brent, and several others nodded in agreement. Feeling much more confident, I went on to the next exhibit—lizard-like creatures from Mars.

The cartoons were a huge hit, especially the UFO slingshot. I couldn't wait until Owen actually finished the whole commercial. When we finished, everyone applauded.

"Excellent job!" Mrs. Driscoll waved us over to give her notes. Quickly, I pulled down our display board so whoever was next could set up, then joined Owen at Mrs. Driscoll's desk. She'd already handed Owen the notes, which I was relieved to see were only one page long.

"I just have a few suggestions on places where you can add more information," she said. "The rides are great, they really make this fun—but the judges will want the majority of your presentation to be scientific, so really focus on the habitats. But overall, this is fantastic!"

"It's the cartoons," I said eagerly. "Wait until you see the whole thing—Owen's not even finished yet!"

Owen blushed, and Mrs. Driscoll smiled at me. "The cartoons are excellent, but so was the rest of the presentation," she said. "You two make a great team!"

I felt my cheeks start to glow, too. "Thanks, Mrs. Driscoll." Following Owen back to our desks, I wondered which of us had the redder face.

Chapter Eight

*T*he mall was swarming Saturday afternoon, probably because we'd been hit with an early heat wave and everyone was trying to escape into the AC. By two o'clock, Julia, Natasha, and I had taken over the dressing rooms at Milanie's, one of our favorite stores. I organized our selections by style into groups while Julia paraded around in a yellow dress with a flared skirt.

"It looks really cute," I said, glancing at her reflection in one of the mirrors. "Not dressy enough for a dance, though."

Julia sighed. "I know. Maybe I can get this one, plus another for the dance." Checking the price tag, she made a face. "Or maybe not."

"Ta-da!" Natasha burst out of one of the rooms and struck a pose. Laughing, I eyed the dress—off the shoulder, floor-length, crimson rosette accents.

"Gorgeous, and too formal."

Natasha grinned. "Yup. Forget the dance, I'm

thinking ahead. Prom." She flipped through the tiered skirts while Julia grabbed a bright pink taffeta dress.

"My vote's still on that green one for you," I told Natasha.

She nodded. "It's my favorite, too, so far."

I'd already tried on four dresses. They were okay, but nothing spectacular. I wasn't sure what I was looking for, though. The idea of going to the dance with Owen was making me more and more nervous. We'd actually be . . . dancing. Like, slow dancing. Back when I'd asked him before winter break, the whole thing had seemed so far in the future, I hadn't even thought about the dancing part.

Now I couldn't *stop* thinking about it.

I also couldn't stop thinking about the dancing penguins in Owen's sketchbook.

Grabbing a turquoise dress with cap sleeves, I glanced from Julia to Natasha. I really wanted to talk to them about Owen, but since I wasn't even sure how I felt, I didn't know exactly what to say.

"I think we're getting the schedule for the science fair this week," I said, holding the dress in front of me. "Fingers crossed none of us get stuck with an early time, since it's the day after the dance. It starts at eight in the morning."

Natasha wrinkled her nose. "Ugh, that'd be annoying. How did you guys do on your presentation in class yesterday, anyway?"

"Really good!" I couldn't help but grin. "Everyone

loved the cartoons. I hope Owen finishes the whole thing this weekend." Trying to keep my voice light, I stepped in front of the mirror. "He's kind of busy working on another project with Ginny."

Julia paused, her arm halfway through a sleeve. "Who's Ginny?"

I kept my eyes on my reflection. "His partner from that art workshop." Smoothing the skirt down, I shook my head. "Nah, I don't like this length." As I turned, I thought I saw Natasha and Julia exchange a glance.

"Owen met a girl there?" Natasha asked lightly.

Nodding, I focused on flipping through more dresses. "They're doing this optional animation project, just for practice. So I guess they talk on the phone and stuff sometimes." Did I sound jealous? I hoped not.

"Oh, that's cool." Julia was silent for a moment. "I'm sure it's nothing to worry about, though."

"I know!" Okay, my voice was definitely too high. "Not that it matters. We're just friends."

"Exactly! It doesn't matter."

I peered at Julia's face in the mirror, checking for signs of sarcasm. But she looked unconcerned. Which kind of made me feel better and worse. Did she mean I had nothing to worry about because there was no way Owen *liked* Ginny? Or did she mean even if he *did* like Ginny, I had nothing to worry about because I didn't like Owen?

Since January, I'd been insisting to Julia and Natasha that I didn't have a crush on Owen. And I hadn't been lying. But now that they finally seemed to believe me . . . well, maybe it wasn't so true anymore.

I knew if I told them about my maybe-crush, they'd get all excited and encourage me to tell Owen. Julia would remind me of how nervous she and Seth were around each other at first, and Natasha would add that I was the one who helped her ask Aaron out.

But this was different. Because Owen wasn't just a boy I knew from band or PE or whatever. Since the beginning of the year, he'd become one of my best friends. If I told him I *liked* him, everything would change between us whether he liked me back or not. Either way, I just wasn't ready for that to happen.

Chewing my lip, I went back to searching through the dresses. I pulled out a silvery one that looked kind of weird on the hanger, but had a pretty wicked geometric pattern covering the skirt. *Cyborg dress*, I thought with a smile, slipping it off the hanger and turning around. Julia was standing in front of the mirror, wearing the bright pink dress.

"Oh!" I exclaimed. "That one. Definitely that one."

Julia beamed. "I think so, too!"

I stepped into a dressing room and quickly pulled on the silver dress. My eyes widened at my reflection.

It was one of those outfits that looked completely different off the hanger. This dress was . . . *cool*. Halter top, flouncy skirt, and the geometric pattern went up the back in silver lace. If it wasn't already a million degrees outside, I'd wear it with my silver combat boots.

But a pair of black sandals would work, too.

I pushed the door open. "Hey, guys, what do you—"

"Oh my *God*!" Natasha cried. "That looks amazing!" She pulled me over to the mirror and spun me around. "Look at the lace on the back! You *have* to wear your hair up to show that off, like this . . ."

Laughing, I waited as she piled my hair on top of my head and clipped a barrette to hold it in place.

Julia clapped. "Perfect! Wow, I don't even remember picking that out!"

"I grabbed it off one of the racks in the back," Natasha said. "But it looks totally different than I thought it would. You've *got* to get this one, Holly," she added fervently, and Julia nodded in agreement.

I grinned, turning back to the mirror. "I will."

After buying our dresses (Julia got the pink taffeta one, and Natasha went with a green dress with spaghetti straps), we walked out into the mall. When we passed the theater, Julia let out a shriek and pointed. Glancing over, I saw the *Mutant Clowns from Planet Z* poster and smiled.

"I meant to warn you about that," I told her. "We saw the preview before *House of the Wicked 2*. It looks really cool, but those clowns are kind of freaky."

"*Kind* of?" Julia repeated incredulously. Natasha was attempting to walk past the theater with her hand over her eyes, which made us laugh. I grabbed the back of her shirt before she wandered onto the escalator, and something in the food court on the first floor caught my eye.

"Maggie Moo's!" I turned to Julia and Natasha, bouncing on my toes. "Oh, let's go see if Chad's girlfriend is working."

I'd kept my promise to Chad so far and hadn't told Mom or Dad about Amy. But it wouldn't technically be breaking our truce if I met her myself.

Maggie's was pretty busy, so while we stood in line I scrutinized the workers: two girls, one boy. I pointed to the girl with short black hair, who was running the register. "Is that her?" I asked. "She looks like she could be related to Trevor."

Julia squinted. "Maybe!"

We ordered our cones, then moved to the register. I grinned when I saw the girl's name tag.

"You're Amy!"

She took my five-dollar bill, eyebrow raised. "Yeah . . . ?"

"I'm Holly Mead," I told her. "Chad's little sister."

Amy's face lit up. "Oh wow, no way!" She rang up Julia and Natasha's orders. "The horror-movie fanatic, huh? Chad told me."

"Seriously?" I couldn't keep the surprise out of my voice. "He talks about me?"

"Yeah!" Smiling, Amy handed Julia her change. "Way to get him to finally clean that car, by the way. That thing was getting out of control."

"Wait, he told you he cleaned it?" I sputtered as

Julia and Natasha started giggling. "I cleaned it!"

Amy snorted. "That doesn't surprise me."

"He can't even do his own laundry," I told her, causing Julia to choke on a mouthful of coconut almond. "He's been paying me to do it for, like, a year."

"Oh my God, Holly, your brother is *so* going to kill you," Natasha said, her eyes wide. But Amy was laughing.

"Also unsurprising." She pointed to an empty table. "Why don't you guys sit down? It looks like we've got a lull coming up."

We plopped our bags on the table and waited while Amy rang up the last few customers in line. My scoop of peanut-butter swirl was starting to melt.

"I cannot believe this," I said. "My brother's girlfriend is actually *cool*. How did this happen?"

"I can't believe you told her you do his laundry." Julia's eyes were still teary from laughter. "You're so dead."

She had a point. Chad wasn't going to be too happy about that. I shrugged, licking my ice cream. "Serves him right for taking the credit on the car cleaning."

Amy dragged a chair over and set a can of soda on the table. "So did you see *House 2*? I keep getting scheduled to work weekends, so I haven't seen it yet."

"I saw it a few weeks ago," I told her. "I went with your brother and some other friends from band. I think you've met Gabby," I added.

"Oh yeah!" Amy grinned. "That girl is freaking

awesome. She drives Trevor nuts, I love it." We giggled as she took a sip of soda. "I remember him griping his head off to Owen when he found out she was going to that movie, too. But then when he got home he couldn't stop laughing about how she threw candy all over the place." Suddenly, her eyes widened and she set the can down with a *thunk*. "Oh, hang on—you're *that* Holly!"

"What?"

Amy's eyes sparkled like she was about to laugh. "Owen's . . . friend."

"Oh. Yeah." My stomach started fluttering.

"He's been Trevor's best friend since, like, forever," Amy said, smiling. "I love Owen." She paused, pressing her lips together. "He talks about you *all* the time."

I almost dropped my cone. "Really?"

"What does he say?" cried Natasha, then closed her mouth when Julia elbowed her in the side. My face was probably reaching a nuclear level of red.

Amy reached for her soda again. "Lots of stuff. All good," she added quickly, winking at me. "Are you two . . . ?"

"Just friends," Julia said, giving me an innocent smile. "Right?"

I focused on my ice cream. "Right."

"Gotcha." Glancing up when a group of teenagers walked in, Amy sighed and got to her feet. "Back to work. I'm so glad you stopped by!" She grinned at me. "Can't wait to tell Chad I met you."

I laughed. "I don't think he's going to be too excited.

But it was great to meet you, too."

When Julia and Natasha headed to the trash cans, Amy leaned in a little closer. "You know, I was friends with Chad for a long time before I asked him out."

"*You* asked *him* out?" I blurted, stopping just short of adding "*why?*"

"Yup. Got impatient," she said with a grin. "Anyway, I'm just saying—I've known Owen forever, and he's always been shy. But I can tell he thinks you're pretty great. So . . ." She shrugged. "Just letting you know, I guess."

Amy gave me a quick, one-armed hug, then ducked back behind the counter. I followed Julia and Natasha back into the mall, feeling more nervous about the dance than ever.

But a little more excited, too.

Chapter Nine

"**W**e should do another fund-raiser."

Mr. Dante glanced up from his computer. I stood in the doorway of his office, wearing my band-concert uniform—a dress with ridiculously puffy sleeves topped with velvet bows that had probably been worn by several generations of reluctant band girls before me.

"A fund-raiser?" Mr. Dante asked.

I nodded emphatically. "For uniforms. You said we have to fake confidence even if we're not really confident, right?" Spreading my arms, I looked down at the scratchy black fabric. "How am I supposed to feel confident in *this*?"

Laughing, Mr. Dante turned back to his monitor. "I see. New uniforms for next year . . . I'll talk to the boosters about it. I think I've got a catalog here somewhere, actually."

My eyes widened. "A catalog for band uniforms, really? Can I see it?"

"We're loading the bus in five minutes," he replied, glancing at the clock. I tried to ignore the twist of nerves in my stomach. Our rehearsals this week had been great, but now that the Thursday morning of UIL had arrived, I was back to freaking out.

"Can I take it on the bus?" I asked. "I swear I'll be careful with it. Please?"

Mr. Dante smiled. "Sure. Nervous?" he added, opening a drawer.

"Um . . ." I fidgeted a little. "Is it okay if I say yes?"

"Of course." Mr. Dante handed me the catalog. "I know UIL is intimidating. But try to have fun, too."

"I will." I glanced at the cover. "Are all of the boys' uniforms tuxes? You should know that not a single guy in this band actually knows how to tie a bow tie. I'm thinking their parents must have helped them before the winter concert or something, because it's kind of catastrophic out there."

Mr. Dante chuckled. "Well, they'd better figure it out. Actually . . ." Squinting, he pointed behind me. "It looks like Gabby's on the case."

I turned to see Gabby attempting to retie Trevor's bow tie, despite his efforts to bat her hands away.

"I know what I'm doing!" she yelled, grabbing his collar. Trevor made a gagging noise. "I do this for my cousins all the time when they—would you hold *still*?"

"Help me!" Trevor choked when he saw me giggling. Behind him, Owen was trying to fix his own bow tie, which stayed resolutely crooked.

Gabby glanced over Trevor's shoulder. "You're next," she told Owen sternly.

Still laughing, I headed to my cubby to get my horn and music. When I came back out into the band hall, a line of boys had formed in front of Gabby. And by the time we loaded the bus, every single bow tie was perfectly straight.

$$\text{\textglorious}$$

I spent the short bus ride to Ridgewood High School huddled over the catalog with Natasha. "Some of these are almost pretty," I said, tapping my pencil on a picture of a girl in a dark blue satin dress with completely normal, non-puffy sleeves.

"Does that one come in red?" Natasha wrinkled her nose. "Oh, it doesn't. We should probably only recommend ones in school colors. Or black, like these." We were writing down a list of our favorite uniforms' item numbers to give Mr. Dante later.

Julia peered over the back of the seat in front of us. "I like the neckline on that one," she said, pointing. "Oh look, the tuxes have red vests to match!"

I added it to the list. "Pretty much all of these are way better than what we've got. I bet our uniforms are the oldest out of the whole district."

But as the bus pulled into the Ridgewood parking lot, I saw that wasn't true. A bunch of kids carrying instruments stood in neat rows on a set of risers set up just outside the main entrance for photos, all wearing dresses and tuxes that looked about as outdated as ours. As they streamed down the riser steps and headed toward a bus, I noticed with a jolt that their director was holding a trophy. *Sweepstakes,* I thought, my stomach knotting up again.

Mrs. Park, one of our booster chaperones, stood up at the front of the bus. "Leave your cases here!" she called. "Make sure you have everything you need—mouthpiece, music, all of that."

Once we parked, I slipped the catalog into my horn case, triple-checked to make sure all my music was in my folder, and followed Natasha off the bus.

We filed across the parking lot and waited outside a side entrance while Mr. Dante went in. Turning, I realized Aaron was right behind me.

"Got your music?" I couldn't help asking teasingly. A few months ago, Aaron had lost his sheet music for a trio we both were in for Solo and Ensemble Competition. He'd only realized it a few minutes before we were supposed to play.

Aaron laughed. "Pretty sure. I checked about five times before we left." He opened his folder, and Natasha leaned past me to look.

"Hey, the pages aren't even wrinkled!" she joked. Aaron grinned at her.

"Shocking, right?"

I smiled. It looked like things were finally getting less awkward between them.

The doors opened, and Mr. Dante waved us inside.

Once we were in the hallway, he and Mrs. Park helped us get into a single-file line by section, and warned us about a hundred times not to talk or make noise, since we'd be walking past the sight-reading room on the way to the warm-up room. When we turned the corner, I noticed a huge dry-erase board hanging on the wall with RATINGS written along the top. A list of middle-school bands were in a column on the left. Someone had already added the ratings for the first several bands that had performed.

The band I'd seen with the Sweepstakes trophy must have been Jacksonville, I realized. Because as of right now, they were literally the *only* band with Superior ratings from all of the judges on the stage and in sight-reading. Craning my neck, I scanned the rest of the ratings before we rounded the next corner. My stomach plummeted.

Most of the bands so far had Excellent ratings in sight-reading, and there were already two that only had Good ratings. The sight-reading piece had to be really hard.

I tried to push that thought out of my mind as we entered the choir room for warm-ups. We took our seats and adjusted the music stands as Mr. Dante pulled the folder with his scores out of his shoulder bag. Owen leaned a little closer to me.

"Did you see those ratings?" he whispered, and my stomach flipped in a way that had nothing to do with UIL nerves.

"Yup," I whispered back. "Barf."

Mr. Dante didn't look worried at all as he led us through our warm-ups. I wondered if he was faking confidence, or if he really *was* confident. Either way, I felt slightly more relaxed by the time we left the choir room and filed onto the stage. I could see the three judges in the mostly empty auditorium—one in the second row, one around the middle, and one in the very back, each with a clipboard and pencil. The guy in the second row was already scribbling away.

A girl in a Ridgewood Band T-shirt stepped in front of the microphone on the side of the stage. After she introduced us and told the judges which songs we'd be playing, she hurried offstage, and Mr. Dante smiled at us.

Try to have fun, too. I sat up straight and lifted my horn.

The march sounded great, but it was also our easiest piece. I realized that was probably the reason we played it first—a confidence booster. It must have worked, too, because the ballad we played next sounded just as good.

"Labyrinthine Dances" was last. I remembered that rehearsal a few weeks ago, when Mr. Dante had reminded us how painfully slow we'd started playing it back in September, and how far we'd come.

We'd been practicing this song for a *year*. It was the most challenging music I'd ever worked on. And that just made it more fun.

As soon as we played the first measure, all my nervousness disappeared. We flew through the music, or at least, that's what it felt like. All those fast rhythms and key changes that used to be so difficult just sounded . . . effortless. By the end, Mr. Dante was beaming. Natasha bounced a little in her chair.

"That was *awesome!*" she whispered. I nodded, unable to stop smiling.

As we left the stage, I squinted at the judges, wondering what they were writing about our performance and if getting lots of comments was a good sign or a bad sign. The butterflies returned full force when I realized all three of them were writing down our rating right now. If two of them gave us a Superior rating, and one gave us an Excellent rating, we'd still have an overall Superior rating for the stage performance. But we wouldn't get that Sweepstakes trophy.

Plus we still had sight-reading. And based on the ratings the bands before us had received, getting three Superior ratings in the sight-reading room would be next to impossible.

Chapter Ten

By the time we'd lined up in the hall, my hands were sweating so badly I thought for sure I was going to drop my horn.

We followed Mr. Dante into the band hall for sight-reading and quietly took our seats. Each music stand already held a piece of sheet music, turned facedown. At the front of the room, three judges sat at a long table, facing us. Weird how this felt more intimidating than being on a stage in front of a huge crowd. *Maybe because onstage, you can't actually see people's faces*, I thought. But these judges were right there behind Mr. Dante, staring at us. I glanced at the judge on the right, a woman with dark gray-streaked hair. She looked familiar, but it wasn't until she looked up that I recognized her.

My all-region band director—Mrs. Collier! I almost waved, then realized that would probably be unprofessional or something. So I just drummed my fingers nervously on the bell of my horn while Mr.

Dante spoke quietly with the judges. Mrs. Collier was a college music professor, I remembered. And she was a lot of fun. It helped me feel slightly less nervous to realize that the judges were actual band directors, not evil robots who just wanted to give low ratings.

I almost laughed out loud. *Evil Robot Band Directors*— that would be a pretty funny cartoon. I'd have to tell Owen about it later.

When the judge on the left stood, I forced myself to focus. He explained the whole sight-reading procedure, and reminded us not to play during Mr. Dante's instruction time. Then Mr. Dante stepped onto the podium and told us to turn our music over.

We did, and I almost fell out of my chair.

They had to be *kidding*. This music was even worse than "Triumphant Fanfare," the song we'd tried to sight-read a few weeks ago. And Mr. Dante said that was as difficult as it was supposed to get.

I glanced from Natasha to Owen—both of them looked as freaked out as I felt. But Mr. Dante appeared completely relaxed, as always.

Fake it, I told myself firmly, and sat up straighter.

"So we start off in the key of concert E flat, with a 3/4 time signature," Mr. Dante began. "If that looks familiar, you're probably thinking of 'Labyrinthine Dances.' In fact, French horns and low brass, take a closer look at that rhythm in measure three—recognize it?"

Squinting at the measure, I smiled. He was right—it was a tricky rhythm, but one we saw a lot in

"Labyrinthine Dances." Maybe this wouldn't be so bad after all.

Mr. Dante talked through the music until the first timer went off. Then he started conducting from the beginning, singing some of our parts while we pressed our keys (or, in the percussionists' case, air-drummed). Suddenly, Mr. Dante stopped.

"Alright, everyone touch measure sixty-four!" he exclaimed. Confused, I put my finger on my music, along with everyone else. Then I saw the coda sign and grinned.

"The curse of the coda," Mr. Dante said solemnly, and several of us giggled. Behind him, I saw Mrs. Collier smile. "Not today. Let's start back at measure fifty-six, first time. So take the repeat, then we'll go through to the end."

He started conducting again, still pointing out things like dynamics and reminding us to look up at him every few measures. When the coda sign came up, he bellowed: "*Coda!*" and everyone, including the judges, laughed. But after the last measure, not a single one of us was still pressing valves or air-drumming. Before Mr. Dante could comment, the timer went off.

"Well," he said with a grin. "All we have to do now is play it."

And we did. Maybe everyone was faking confidence like me, or maybe we really *were* confident after all. Either way, the beginning sounded great—even the tricky rhythm in measure three. And while there were a few mistakes or wrong notes here and there, we stayed together and played in tune. When the coda came up, Mr. Dante gave us a giant, almost comical cue. After the final note, we all froze, including Mr. Dante. There were a few seconds of dead silence. Then Mr. Dante lowered his hands and gave us a thumbs-up.

No one spoke until we were out in the hall, when everyone started chattering at once.

"That was good, right?" I asked Natasha and Owen. "I mean, it wasn't perfect, but . . ."

"It was better than a lot of our rehearsals," Owen said. "And the music was really hard."

Making a face, I pointed at the ratings board as we passed it. "Yeah, but the judges don't seem to care about that." Jacksonville was still the only band with Sweepstakes. None of our ratings were posted yet, but two more bands had been added. Both of them had Superior ratings on stage, but only Excellent ratings in sight-reading.

Outside the main entrance, a few teachers in Ridgewood High School T-shirts were waiting to organize us on the risers for our group picture. By the time I'd squeezed between Natasha and Owen on the third row, I realized Mr. Dante was gone.

"He's getting our ratings," said Brooke, who stood next to Owen. I remembered how the Jacksonville band director had been carrying a Sweepstakes trophy when they'd taken their picture. Natasha let out a little squeak that was half-excited, half-terrified.

"Don't worry," Brooke told us. "We sounded great." But I noticed her eyes kept flicking to the entrance.

The Ridgewood teachers tried to help the photographer organize us for the picture, which turned out to be kind of a challenge. Trevor forgot to lock his trombone slide, and the whole thing slid off and fell between the steps and under the risers. In the front row, Leah Collins kept nervously flipping her drumsticks and accidentally bashed Sophie in the nose. And every few seconds, someone would stand on their tiptoes to see if Mr. Dante was coming yet. I was in the middle of telling Owen about my *Evil Robot Band Directors* idea when Gabby yelled: "There he is!"

"Oh no," Natasha said softly. "I don't see a trophy."

My stomach plummeted. In a few seconds, I went from thinking we'd played great to feeling positive we'd somehow set a record for the worst ratings ever both onstage and in sight-reading.

"He did this on the band trip, though—hid the trophy behind his back," Gabby said, although her voice was doubtful.

Everyone fell silent as Mr. Dante stepped in front of the risers, setting his bag on the ground. I groaned inwardly—no hands behind his back this time.

"First of all, I want to tell you how proud I am of all your hard work this year," Mr. Dante said. "I know I really pushed you, especially with 'Labyrinthine

Dances,' but I'm amazed at how far you've come. And after our performance onstage, I was completely unsurprised to see that all three judges gave us a Superior rating!"

Several people cheered a little, but I barely managed a smile. I mean, I was excited, but we'd worked so hard on sight-reading, too. If the music hadn't been quite so hard, I bet we'd have gotten Superior ratings, no problem. It didn't really seem fair.

"I'm also very impressed with your performance in the sight-reading room," Mr. Dante continued. "I'm sure some of you noticed the ratings board. The sight-reading music was more challenging than usual this year, which made it difficult for any band to receive a Superior rating—particularly from all three judges. But I feel like we played the best we could." Pausing, Mr. Dante smiled at us. "Which makes getting Sweepstakes even better."

He pulled the trophy out of his bag and held it up, and the band *exploded*.

That's what it must've sounded like from across the parking lot, at least. Over all the noise, I could hear Gabby yelling "That was totally evil!" at Mr. Dante, who was laughing. I hugged Owen right before Julia hopped up two rows and tackled me, Natasha, and Gabby. It took the poor photographer several minutes to get everyone back in our positions on the risers. Mr. Dante stood next to the front row, holding our Sweepstakes trophy.

"Ready?" The photographer stood behind his camera. "I'd say *smile,* but that seems pretty unnecessary," he joked, and we laughed. He was right, though. Five minutes later when our bus pulled out of the parking lot, I was still smiling so hard my cheeks hurt.

Chapter Eleven

$\mathcal{T}$he expressions of the workers behind the pizza buffet at Spins were kind of funny. Probably because about forty kids in tuxes and ugly puffy-sleeved dresses just had burst through the doors, yelling and jumping around like we were all on a sugar rush. (Which most of us were, thanks to the massive bag of celebratory M&M's Gabby had opened on the bus.)

Gabby skipped the pizza and went straight to the cinnamon sticks, piling her plate high before claiming a massive circular booth in the corner. Victoria and Max joined her, along with Trevor and Owen. Julia and Natasha hurried over to sit next to Victoria, so the only spot left for me was on the end next to Owen. Which I was pretty sure had been intentional, judging from their too-innocent looks.

"What's your deal with dessert, anyway?" Trevor asked Gabby around a mouthful of pizza. "Don't you ever eat real food?"

With an exaggerated, weary sigh, Gabby leaned back. "Trevor, I'm going to tell you a story," she announced. "It's called 'Death by Tofu-Spinach Scramble.' Once upon a time, there was a girl whose mother thought sugar was the source of all evil, so she banned it from the kingdom. She—"

"The *kingdom*?" Victoria interrupted with a grin, while the rest of us snickered.

Gabby nodded solemnly. "Yes, the Kingdom of Flores. A magical place where peanut-butter cups grew on trees and it rained Jolly Ranchers, until the queen was brainwashed by her diet support group and decided everyone in the kingdom should live off lettuce and carrots, like rabbits."

Brandishing her cinnamon stick like a wand, Gabby explained how the queen had used magic to turn chocolate into tofu and Twizzlers into celery sticks, until Princess Flores, who suffered from severe health-food allergies and needed sugar as an antidote, was forced to become a candy-hunting outlaw. By the time she got to the part where the princess barely survived a quest for life-saving cinnamon sticks after a deadly tofu-spinach breakfast, everyone was laughing almost too much to eat. Even Trevor.

"I definitely need some dessert after that," Natasha said, still giggling. She slid out of the booth, and Julia followed.

As soon as the others started talking again, Owen turned to me, his eyes bright. "Guess what?" he said, continuing before I could respond. "My parents are sending me to an art camp this summer! It's not animation, though, mostly drawing and illustrating. But the teacher is a real comic-book artist!"

I couldn't help but grin, because he looked so excited. "That's so cool! Where is it?"

"This school near Dallas," Owen said. "Two whole weeks, too. It's in July."

"Wow!" I tried to sound enthusiastic, but it was hard with my brain screaming *Hang on—isn't Ginny from Dallas?*

I listened to Owen describe the camp, smiling and nodding and wondering whether or not Ginny the Amazing Artist would be there, too. For two whole weeks. With Owen.

Ugh.

After a few minutes, I got up to refill my drink. No matter how hard I tried not to, I couldn't help feeling jealous of Ginny. Which was ridiculous for about a million reasons. I mean, I didn't even know if she'd be at that art camp. And even if she *was*, that didn't mean Owen liked her. And even if he *did*, Owen wasn't my boyfriend.

I stood in front of the soda fountain, lost in thought, until my cup started overflowing with root beer.

"Oops!" Making a face, I pulled the cup away too late.

"Here you go!"

Glancing up, I realized Aaron was next to me,

holding out a napkin. "Oh! Thanks," I said, taking it and wiping off my cup.

"No problem." Aaron started filling his own cup with ice. "So I saw *House 2* last weekend."

"Yeah?" I dried my hand and tossed the sopping napkin in the trash. "I saw it a few weeks ago. I loved it."

He nodded. "Me too. Although I think I still like the first one better."

"Really?" I asked. "I thought this one was scarier."

"It was, but . . ." Aaron looked thoughtful. "I don't know. I guess I liked the ending of the first one more."

I laughed. "Why, because in the second one the girl turned out to be hallucinating?"

"Well, yeah!" Aaron said earnestly. "I mean, in the first movie the ghosts were all real. The house was actually haunted. That's what made it so creepy."

"That's what Owen said!" I shook my head. "I think it's creepier that she was imagining it in the second one. Doesn't it freak you out that she was so sure everything that happened in the second movie was real? It's like the ghosts from the first movie were actually in her head! The house wasn't haunted—*she* was."

We debated for a few more minutes, but I was pretty sure Aaron still thought the first movie was better. He wasn't alone—I'd had this argument with pretty much everyone. The only person who agreed with me was Chad. My brother might be annoying sometimes, but at least he really *got* horror like I did.

Still, talking to Aaron was fun, and I was smiling

by the time I went back to my seat. But as soon as I saw Owen, I remembered the whole Ginny thing, and my stomach dropped a little. Maybe I should just ask him flat-out if she was going to be at that camp. Was there a way to do it without sounding like a jealous nutcase? Taking a deep breath, I turned to Owen.

"Cinnamon stick?" he asked, offering me his plate.

"Thanks!" I took one, but set it on my napkin without taking a bite. Owen spoke again before I could say anything.

"Are you still coming over after school? I finished the cartoon last night."

"Yeah!" I nodded. "I can't wait to see it. And . . ." I paused, still trying to think of a way to ask about Ginny.

Suddenly, I felt seriously annoyed with myself. What was my problem? So what if Owen was friends with this girl? And so what if she was a great artist, too? Or if they talked on the phone? I talked to Aaron about horror movies and stuff a lot, because he was my friend. Even if Owen and I were dating, there would be nothing wrong with that.

I realized Owen was still waiting for me to speak. "And, um . . . maybe afterward we can get some *Prophets* time?" I asked. "It's been a while." *Prophet Wars* was our favorite video game, although thanks to all our homework and projects, we hadn't been able to play much since before spring break.

Owen perked up. "Yeah! I forgot to tell you— they're releasing an expansion pack next month! Ten new levels, plus a bunch of new weapons and add-ons for the tanks."

"Really?" I said excitedly. "Should we order it? We can split the cost."

"Maybe," Owen replied, smiling. "It's still pretty expensive, and my mom just bought me that tablet and everything after the workshop. But I'll ask her."

"I'll ask mine, too." I picked up the cinnamon stick and took a bite. Maybe sugar was the antidote for jealousy, too, because I suddenly felt a hundred times better.

$\oint$

We got back to school halfway through fifth period. Owen and I barely had time to set up for the lab assignment Mrs. Driscoll had given before the bell rang. During seventh-period announcements, the assistant principal mentioned the band's UIL Sweepstakes, and Julia and I did little happy dances behind our computers.

"I can't believe UIL is over," I said, picturing the Summer Countdown Calendar on my bulletin board. "Just the science fair and the concert left. And finals, I guess."

Julia cleared her throat. "And the *dance*."

I grinned. "Yeah, that too."

"Oh hey!" Julia said, eyes wide. "Why don't you and Owen come to dinner with me and Seth before the dance? My parents are taking us to some fancy place my dad loves. They won't sit with us, though," she added hastily. "They promised we could get our own table."

My heart gave an extra-hard thump. "That would be fun! I'll ask Owen after school." And I meant it—going to dinner with Julia and Seth *would* be fun. It would also very much feel like a double date.

After school, I met Owen near the front entrance to walk to his house. We talked about the science fair the whole time. When Mrs. Driscoll had given us the handout last semester, Owen had been way more excited than me. But now, I was looking forward to it just as much as he was. Our project really was cool. And after I saw the finished cartoon, I was totally convinced we were going to win.

"Play it again!" I yelled, bouncing up and down on my toes in front of Owen's computer. Laughing, he tapped the space bar.

Coming Soon . . . Alien Park! flashed across the screen, and our commercial started again. Owen had added a soundtrack and a bunch of funny sound effects to accompany the cartoon aliens swimming in the Europa habitat, crawling around the Mars exhibit, and zipping around the Saturn roller coaster.

"Hang on, pause!" I said suddenly, leaning forward. Owen hit the space bar again, stopping on the UFO slingshot. All of the aliens inside were different—blue, purple, and orange skin, some with tentacles, some with regular arms and hands. And in the very front were two green aliens: a blond boy and a girl with a brown ponytail.

"Is that *us?*" I cried. "Did you make us aliens?"

Owen was smiling, his cheeks a little pink. "Yeah. I was wondering if you'd notice. I figured since we can't actually visit Alien Park, this is the next best thing."

For a few seconds, I just gaped at the screen. "That . . . ," I finally managed to say. "Is. Amazing."

"Thanks." Owen looked both pleased and embarrassed. He hit PLAY, and we watched the rest of the cartoon. The second it finished, I turned to face him.

"Do you want to go to dinner before the dance Friday?" I blurted out. "Julia's parents can take us with them. I mean, not with *them*. With Julia and . . ." I stopped, shaking my head. Owen was blinking like crazy. "Okay, starting over. Julia and Seth are going to dinner before the dance, and she invited us to go with them, if you want."

"Oh," said Owen. "Okay! That sounds fun."

"Okay, it's a date!" As soon as I said it, I winced. "I mean, um . . . you know. For dinner. Anyway . . . *Prophets?*" I walked over to the sofa, mostly so he couldn't see me blushing.

"Sure." Owen plugged the controllers into the console while I mentally chewed myself out. It's a *date?* Seriously? Why, brain, *why?* I chanced a peek at Owen. Still red-faced, like me.

He's always been shy, Amy had told me. She was definitely right about that. But I'd never been all that shy. And yet any time Owen and I got anywhere near the subject of dating, I turned into Queen Awkward and did things like spit soda all over his kitchen or stammer or turn tomato red.

After ten minutes of blowing up alien pods, everything felt back to normal. We joked around and got to level nineteen and laughed when Owen's tank got stuck in a nuclear swamp. It was easy and not awkward at all. I didn't want it to change.

But I couldn't ignore the fact that my maybe-crush on Owen was getting a lot less "maybe."

Chapter Twelve

The week after UIL flew by. I turned in my research paper on Eleanor Roosevelt to Mr. Franks on Monday, finished my group history project on Tuesday, and did my computer-lab PowerPoint presentation on Wednesday. When I found out on Friday that I'd gotten an A on both my math quiz and my Spanish brochure, I started to think maybe I'd survive my classes this semester after all.

I spent most of Friday afternoon getting ready for the science fair the next day. Mrs. Driscoll had given us the schedule earlier in the week, and Owen and I had lucked out—we wouldn't present Alien Park until after lunch. Julia had an afternoon slot, too. But poor Natasha had gotten stuck with her presentation at nine in the morning.

When I finished triple-checking my notecards, I stood and looked around my room for another distraction. My eyes fell on the book Julia had loaned me weeks ago, lying on my dresser. Grabbing it, I flopped down on my bed and started to read, trying to ignore the butterfly colony that was apparently making a new home in my stomach.

Nearly an hour later, I sat up with a jolt, like an alarm had gone off. But it was just the muffled thump of loud music coming from Chad's room. I glanced at the clock—Owen's mom was dropping him off in about an hour, and Julia's dad was picking us up here for dinner. I said a silent prayer my brother would stay in his room until we were gone.

I took a quick shower, then headed downstairs to get Mom's help with my hair and makeup. Back in my room, I got dressed, slipping on my sandals just as the doorbell rang. I hurried down the hall, crossing my fingers as I passed Chad's room, and reached the bottom of the stairs just as Mom opened the front door.

"Come on in!" she said brightly. "Owen, don't you look nice. Teresa, I feel like I haven't seen you in ages!"

Mrs. Grady stepped inside, followed by Owen. "I know, same here! Oh, Holly—that dress is *adorable*."

"Thanks. It's a cyborg dress," I said without thinking.

Mom quirked an eyebrow. "A *what?*"

Blushing, I shrugged. "I don't know. That's just what I thought when I picked it out."

"Well, I think it's lovely," Mrs. Grady said with a laugh. A few seconds passed with her and Mom just standing there staring at me and Owen with big, dorky smiles. Then Mom offered Mrs. Grady a cup of coffee and they disappeared into the kitchen, leaving us in the foyer. Relieved, I hopped off the last step and smiled at him.

"Nice suit!" I said. It was, too. His dark gray suit and tie with a blue shirt looked infinitely cooler than the band tux, that was for sure. My stupid stomach-butterflies were flapping around like crazy.

"Thanks," said Owen. His voice sounded funny, although mine probably did, too. "Um . . . did you call it a cyborg dress?"

I glanced down at the skirt. "Yeah. I guess it's the silver and all the shapes. Kind of a weird dress, but I like it."

"Me too." Owen hesitated, then added, "You look really pretty."

He said it so fast, I almost missed it. My face started to heat up again.

"Thank you."

We both looked down, and I realized he was holding a corsage. "Is that for me?"

Blinking, Owen stared at his hand. "Oh! Yeah."

I slipped the corsage on my wrist. The flower was the same shade of blue as Owen's shirt, surrounded by tiny white buds. "Thanks!"

"You're welcome."

When the doorbell rang again, I was pretty sure Owen was as relieved as me. Our moms came out of the kitchen just as I let Julia and Seth in, along with

Julia's parents. Mr. Gordon had brought his camera, and despite Julia's protests, insisted on taking about a million pictures of the four of us. Which was actually kind of fun, even though our parents couldn't seem to stop using words like "cute" and "sweet." Every time they did, Julia and I would make faces at each other. Having her there made me a lot less nervous.

Until Chad appeared at the top of the stairs.

He stopped halfway down, looking around the crowded foyer in confusion. When he saw me standing next to Owen, he smirked.

Fortunately, Mom saw him, too. "What time are you working till tonight, Chad?" she asked before he could say anything.

"Uh . . ." Chad squinted at her. "Nine thirty, I think."

"Perfect!" Mom smiled as Mr. Gordon snapped another picture of Julia and Seth in front of the window. "Dad and I were planning on going out for ice cream later, if you want to meet us at Maggie's."

Chad and I both gaped at her. Then Chad turned to me, and I held out my hands, palms flat.

"Holly—"

"I didn't say *anything*," I interrupted. "I swear."

"She didn't." Mom waved a cell phone at Chad. "You *really* need to stop leaving this thing lying around, hon. Anyway, I can't wait to meet this . . ." She glanced at the screen. "Amy."

I pressed my lips together hard to keep from laughing. Julia grinned at me. "She's really nice, Mrs.

Mead," she said innocently. "You'll like her."

"I'm sure I will." Mom smiled at Chad, who looked like he wanted to shout at someone, but he wasn't sure who.

I leaned closer to Owen. "I probably shouldn't remind her to tell Amy the cowboy-boot story, huh?" I asked in a low voice. Owen laughed, but stopped quickly when Chad shot us a death glare.

When Julia reminded her dad we had a dinner reservation, he finally pocketed his camera and we headed outside. "Have fun!" Mom called. Turning, I smiled at Chad.

"You too! Say hi to Amy for me!"

The look on his face gave Julia and me the giggles for pretty much the whole car ride.

$\oint$

Not only did Mr. and Mrs. Gordon sit at their own table, but they were in a whole different room. Nita's Bistro was definitely the fanciest restaurant I'd ever been to, with chandeliers and flowers and candles on the tables. My eyes bulged when I saw the prices on the menu.

"My parents are paying," Julia said when she noticed my expression. "I'm pretty sure my dad called all of your parents earlier. He really just wanted an excuse to eat here," she added, grinning. "I think he'd come once a week if he could, but my mom says they have to save it for 'special occasions.'"

Even though we were all dressed up in a super-romantic restaurant, after a few minutes I realized it didn't feel much different than sitting at the cafeteria table together. In fact, for a while I forgot to be nervous about the whole "date" thing.

"I finally started reading that book," I told Julia, twirling pasta on my fork. "I seriously cannot believe you like it."

Julia's eyes widened. "You mean you don't?"

"No, I love it!" I said. "It's just a lot scarier than you said it'd be."

"But it's funny, too!" Julia grabbed a piece of bread. "That's why I kept reading, I guess."

I put my fork down. "So that's the secret to getting you into horror! It just has to be funny, too."

"There's a movie coming out this summer that's kind of comedy and horror," Owen told Julia. "*Mutant Clowns from Planet—*"

"No!" Julia cried, shaking her head frantically as Seth and I snickered. "No, no, no, no way, *no*. Never."

Owen blinked. "Why not?"

"She's afraid of clowns," I explained, and Seth nodded.

"Serious phobia."

Julia rolled her eyes. "It's not a *phobia*."

"It is," Seth said. "*Coulrophobia.* I looked it up after you saw that clown making animal balloons at my cousin's birthday party and freaked out."

I choked a little on my pasta. "What happened?"

"I didn't freak out," Julia protested. "I just . . . left the room."

Seth caught my eye and grinned. "She hid in the coat closet."

I giggled, and Julia rolled her eyes. "Look, a fear of clowns is perfectly healthy, considering they're pure evil."

Owen was still staring at her in disbelief. "Normal clowns, though? The nice ones with painted faces and red noses and—"

"Stop!" Julia yelled, clamping her hands over her ears.

"Okay, no more clown talk," I said, still laughing. "I promise."

After a piece of molten chocolate cake that made me realize why Mr. Gordon loved this restaurant so much, we headed back out to their SUV. Julia slipped her hand into Seth's, patting her belly with her other hand.

"Ugh," she said. "I might be too full to dance!"

I laughed, but just hearing the word *dance* was enough to set my butterflies fluttering around again. When Mr. Gordon pulled into the school parking lot, Julia and Seth hopped out first. Owen went next, then held out his hand to help me out. And even after I'd closed the door behind me, he didn't let go.

Neither of us said a word about it. We just followed Julia and Seth inside, hand in hand like we did it all the time. Julia didn't say anything, either, although I caught the smile on her face when she noticed.

I could hear the thump of the music coming from the gym all the way down the hall, although some of it might have been my heart pounding in my ears. This dance was going to be interesting.

Chapter Thirteen

*J*ust like at the winter dance, I thought it was kind of amazing that some flashing lights and streamers made the gym look so un-gym-like. But as my eyes adjusted to the dim light, I realized the student council had done an even better job this time.

"Wow!" I said, blinking. Glow-in-the-dark moons and stars hung from the high ceiling at different lengths, some of them just a foot or two over our heads. The fluorescent streamers and balloons everywhere all seemed to glow, too. I squinted at the giant lights set up near the DJ.

"Black lights!" Brooke appeared next to us, smiling widely and carrying what looked like a hundred glow necklaces and bracelets in neon colors. "What do you think?"

"It looks amazing!" Julia exclaimed, taking a few necklaces and putting them on. "This is so cool."

I took a purple necklace, then slipped on a matching

bracelet. On my other wrist, the tiny white buds around the blue flower glowed, too. "You guys did an awesome job," I told Brooke. She was student-council president, which seemed like a ton of work. Although I had to admit the idea of organizing a *dance* sounded like pretty much the most fun thing ever.

"Thanks!" Brooke gave Seth and Owen their necklaces. "We were freaking out for a while because our budget was smaller than it was for the winter dance. Then I talked to Mrs. Sutton and she told me the theater department had those black lights. So I ordered a bunch of UV balloons, and all the other glow-in-the-dark stuff was pretty cheap." She gazed around the gym, clearly pleased. "It worked out, I guess."

I nodded. "It totally did. It looks really . . . alien."

Brooke laughed. "I'll take that as a compliment."

"It is," Owen assured her. We'd dropped hands to put on the necklaces and bracelets, which was disappointing. So when the four of us started to make our way across the gym, I took his hand again before I could lose my nerve. It was hard to tell with all the weird lighting, but I was pretty sure I caught a little smile on his face. And more than a few blinks.

"You guys, how happy am I that I wore a white dress?"

Turning, we started to laugh. Gabby spread her arms out so we could get the full effect—between her bright white off-the-shoulder dress and the dozens of glow necklaces and bracelets around her neck and arms, she was practically blinding. She'd even stuck a few glow sticks in her hair, which was twisted up in a bun.

"You look radiant," Seth deadpanned, and Gabby beamed.

"Why, thank you!"

Someone bumped my hip, and I glanced over to see Natasha at my side. "That dress still rocks," she announced.

"Yours too. Nice touch," I added, pointing at the green glow necklaces she was using as a headband. It actually looked really cool with her green dress.

"Thanks!" Natasha leaned closer. "So what's going on here?" she asked in a low voice, glancing pointedly at my and Owen's hands.

I smiled and shrugged, hoping the dim lighting hid my blush. "I don't know. Nothing. Something. Maybe."

Natasha's eyes lit up. "Maybe?" She looked like she wanted to say something else, then changed her mind and just stood wearing a completely goofy grin that made me laugh.

Something about acknowledging it out loud made me feel a lot braver about the whole thing. In fact, with the black lights and glow necklaces making everyone look kind of surreal, I forgot all about my nerves.

"Wanna dance?" I asked Owen.

He grinned. "Yeah."

For almost half an hour, the DJ played nothing but fast songs. During a really upbeat one by Infinite Crush,

Julia's favorite band, Brooke released a black net none of us had noticed overhead, sending dozens of glowing UV balloons onto the dance floor. We danced in a big group, with Gabby and Victoria occasionally doing one of their funny routines while Max and Trevor batted balloons around like volleyballs. I started to think it was kind of silly that any of us even bothered asking dates. We were all together, anyway, so why did it matter?

Then a slow song started. Flushed and out of breath, I glanced at Owen. He smiled nervously.

Oh right. That's why.

Kicking a balloon out of the way, I stepped closer to him while everyone paired up around us. We hesitated for a second. Then I put my hands on his shoulders, and he put his hands on my waist, and we were dancing.

Our faces were pretty close, which was both nice and terrifying. I tried to think of something to talk about, but my mind had gone completely blank. Just when the silence started to make me feel panicky, a glowing pink balloon sailed over and bopped me in the head.

Owen swatted it away. We started laughing, and everything felt normal again.

Relieved, I glanced around and grinned. "Oh, no way—look at that." We turned slowly until Owen was facing Gabby and Trevor, who were dancing together. His eyes widened in surprise.

"That's . . . weird," he said. "I thought they couldn't stand each other."

"I'm not sure," I replied, squinting through the neon stars at Gabby. "I kind of think they like pretending they don't like each other, if that makes sense."

"Huh." Owen laughed a little. "It looks like they're arguing already."

He was right—they were definitely bickering about something. I saw Gabby lightly swat the back of Trevor's head. "But they're still dancing," I pointed out, giggling. "See what I mean?"

When a fast song started up, I was a little disappointed. But it wasn't long before the DJ played a slow one again. For almost an hour, hardly anyone left the dance floor. I saw Natasha dancing with Seth for one song, and with Gabe for two others. Gabby danced with Liam (then Max, then some guy I didn't know, then Victoria). But Owen and I danced together for every slow song. By the fourth or fifth one, I was starting to think maybe dating Owen wouldn't change everything as drastically as I'd thought. After all, I'd been really nervous about dancing with him, but it already felt as normal as just hanging out and playing video games. Well, maybe not *that* normal. But pretty close.

The problem was, I had no idea how to actually tell him all of this. And it might have been my imagination, but it seemed like maybe Owen was thinking the same thing. A few times, he looked like he was going to say something, but stopped himself.

"Want a drink?" he asked when another slow song faded out.

"Sure!"

Dodging a few rogue balloons, we left the dance floor and headed over to the food table. I spotted Aaron and his girlfriend over by the snacks and looked around for Natasha out of habit. She was dancing with Gabe. Again. *Interesting,* I thought with a smile, making a mental note to ask her about that later.

Owen and I wandered around the gym for a few songs, sipping punch and talking about movies and the science fair and pretty much everything except what I really *wanted* to talk about. We were holding hands again, though. Which was starting to get kind of funny, since we seemed to be pretending it didn't mean anything. I had the sudden, ridiculous mental image of us at the dance next year as eighth-graders, holding hands and dancing but insisting to everyone that we were still just friends! It would've made me laugh if it wasn't so pathetic.

I tossed my cup in a trash can as another slow song started. But before Owen and I made it back to the dance floor, Gabby appeared in front of us wearing twice as many glow necklaces as she had been half an hour ago.

"My eyes!" I cried, shielding my face with my free hand.

Gabby grinned. "I found a box of extras on the side of the bleachers. Anyway, you guys mind if I cut in for a dance?"

I glanced at Owen, who looked as surprised as I

felt. "Sure," we both said at the same time, although I couldn't help feeling a little disappointed. Gabby dancing with Owen didn't bother me at all, but I wasn't sure how many songs were left.

Then Gabby grabbed my hand with a bright smile. "I'll have her back in one piece!" she promised Owen. He laughed as she tugged me through the crowd of dancing couples, all the way to the middle of the floor. Gabby spun me around before putting one hand on my back, the other clasping mine out to the side like we were ballroom dancing. Except not as formal, because I couldn't stop giggling.

After a few seconds, Gabby cleared her throat expectantly. "Well?"

"Well what?" I asked, still grinning.

"You like Owen."

She raised an eyebrow, clearly waiting for denial. Tilting my head, I pretended to consider it. Then I said: "Yeah, I do. A lot."

Gabby's eyes widened. Tilting her head back, she yelled *"finally!"* at the ceiling, causing several nearby couples to give us weird looks, including Sophie and Liam. Giggling, I gestured at Gabby to keep her voice down. (Sophie was nice and all, but she was still pretty gossipy. The last thing I wanted was for Owen to hear about this conversation before I could tell him myself how I felt.)

"So have you talked to him yet?" Gabby asked eagerly, waving her hand as a yellow balloon soared over our heads.

"No. Hey, it's hard!" I added in a low voice when she rolled her eyes.

"*I like you.*" Gabby's face was dead serious. "Yeah, you're right. That's super hard to say."

I sighed. "You know what I mean."

"Okay, so don't *say* anything. Get my drift?" Gabby puckered her lips in an exaggerated kiss. I burst into giggles again, feeling my face heat up.

"I can't just . . . do that."

"Oh, sure you can," Gabby said dismissively. "You've got to do something. Or he does. Seriously, watching you two is like the race of the lovesick turtles or something." She started to lead me in a ridiculously slow sort of tango, which just made me crack up again (and earned us a lot more weird looks). "Trevor says he pretty much never stops talking about you," she added, after twirling me around until I felt a little dizzy. "It drives him nuts."

I blushed again, remembering how Amy had said the same thing. "Kind of like how you keep talking about Trevor?"

Gabby snorted. "Quit changing the subject."

"I saw you guys dancing earlier," I went on anyway. "Who asked who?"

"I asked him," Gabby said. "And I will *not* be asking him again."

"Why?"

"Because he got pretty annoyed when I did this." Without warning, Gabby dipped me so low, I thought

I was going to fall flat on my back. I grabbed her shoulders, laughing as she pulled me back up.

"Did you for real?" I managed to choke out, still sniggering.

Gabby smiled proudly. "Of course. I always lead."

I wiped my eyes. "You have no idea how much I wish I'd seen that."

"It was pretty epic," Gabby agreed. "But taking the lead is fun sometimes." She gave me a pointed look. "Know what I mean?"

I nodded. "Yes, Captain Obvious." But despite my light tone, I appreciated Gabby's advice. I liked Owen, so I should tell him. It didn't have to be so complicated.

"You know what, Gabby?" I said. "You're a really good friend. And a great dancer."

Gabby beamed. "You too." She twirled me around one more time as the song ended. When a fast beat started up, the dance floor got a lot more crowded. I spotted Julia and Seth and the others, and Gabby and I made our way over to them. Soon we were in a group again, dancing and batting the balloons all over the place.

Then the DJ announced the last song. While we danced, I told Owen about Gabby and Trevor. "He's probably hiding from her," I finished, snickering. But Owen's eyes were wide.

"Actually . . ." He turned us until I saw Gabby and Trevor not far away, dancing and bickering again. My mouth fell open.

"Well." I shook my head. "Guess I was wrong."

We started talking about the science fair, but I was distracted. *Just tell him,* I thought over and over. But surrounded by our friends on a crowded dance floor, I suddenly felt like everyone was staring at us. Or listening. They weren't, of course, but I didn't want to tell Owen how I felt while crammed in a gym with half the school.

Tomorrow, I decided as the song ended. *Right after the science fair. No chickening out this time.*

Chapter Fourteen

J woke up late Saturday morning after dreaming about a glowing pink spaceship covered in giant speakers blasting "Labyrinthine Dances" while dozens of aliens danced the tango around it. It had to be pretty much the nerdiest dream ever, I decided as I made my bed.

"Well, you're looking cheerful," said Mom when I walked into the kitchen. "The dance was fun, I take it?"

"Yes. Very." I stuck my head into the fridge in a preemptive strike against blushing, pretending to look for the milk. I literally couldn't make my mouth stop smiling.

"Sorry I wasn't awake when you got home," Mom said, cupping her hands around a mug of coffee. "All the ice cream made me sleepy. Dad said you came in wearing glow sticks or something?"

I giggled. "Yeah, the student council handed them out. There was glow stuff everywhere." Grabbing a box of cereal from the pantry, I suddenly remembered my parents' plans yesterday. "Wait, so you went to Maggie's?" I asked eagerly. "Was Amy there?"

"Oh, even better." Mom gave me a rather evil grin. "Not only was she working, her father had just stopped in to pick up an ice-cream cake. We ended up having a nice time chatting with him. Although for some reason Chad looked a little freaked out when he showed up after work and found the four of us at a table together."

Milk sloshed out of my cereal bowl, and I set the carton down quickly. "Are you serious?"

Mom nodded. "I don't know why. What's so intimidating about walking into an ice-cream shop to find your parents hanging out with your girlfriend and her father? And I was telling them such nice stories about him, too."

I started giggling uncontrollably. "Which stories? Please say the cowboy boots."

"Ah, the cowboy boots!" Making a face, Mom took a sip of coffee. "Totally forgot that one. I did tell them about his excellent performance as Captain Hook when he did that play in elementary school. Amy seemed pretty excited when I told her we had it on video. I think we might watch it when she comes over for dinner."

"She's coming over, really?" I asked, grinning. "Awesome. Poor Chad."

Mom snorted. "Poor Chad, nothing. He's been dating that girl since February! It's about time we all got to know her."

"And show her embarrassing videos," I agreed. "That'll be fun. I like Amy."

"Me too," Mom agreed. She paused, eyeing me over her mug. "So will we be inviting Owen over for a family dinner anytime soon?"

I choked on my cereal. "What? Why? I mean sure, I don't . . ." My face got all hot again. "That's different! You and Dad have met Owen tons of times. And he's not my . . . we're not . . ."

Mom gave me a look that was half-sympathetic, half-teasing. "You're not . . . ?"

"He's not my boyfriend," I said, fiddling with my spoon. "Although, um . . . I do like him." Saying it out loud again made me smile, despite my embarrassment. I glanced up to see Mom wearing a very phony expression of surprise.

"That is brand-new information!" she exclaimed, eyes wide. "I had no idea! I can't—"

"Okay, okay!" I said, giggling. "How did you know?"

Mom laughed. "Oh jeez, Holly, let's see. Well, it certainly wasn't that you've been going over to his house every week since September. And it wasn't that time we made fortune cookies so you could slip that little note about the spring dance into one just for him, or the fact that you went to most of his baseball games even though you said it's the most boring game on earth, or that you spent half our vacation at the lake talking about the art contest he'd won, or framed that lovely picture he—"

She stopped, batting away the napkin I'd thrown at her. "Fine," I said, still smiling. "But I really haven't had a crush on him the whole year. He's my friend, and . . ." I paused, staring at my cereal. "I guess that's why I'm kind of nervous about telling him."

Standing, Mom headed over to the coffee pot. "So you *are* going to tell him?"

"I think so, yeah."

She smiled, pouring another cup. "Good."

I waited for her to say something else. "That's it? No advice? What if everything changes and gets all weird? What if—"

Mom waved her hand dismissively. "Holly, let me ask you this," she said, sitting down again. "Let's say you'd gone with Owen to that dance right before Christmas. Would it have been the same as last night?"

I started to say yes, then stopped. Because I remembered the winter dance, how I'd still had a crush on Aaron. Owen and I definitely would've had fun together, but we wouldn't have walked around holding hands or anything. We didn't *like* each other then. The dance yesterday, on the other hand . . .

"See what I mean?" Mom said. "You're worried about things changing, but they've already changed without you even noticing. You'd be surprised how often that happens," she added, glancing at the clock. "Doesn't Chad's shift start at noon? That boy really needs to learn how to set an alarm."

While Mom rinsed out her coffee mug, I thought

about what she'd said. It was funny—I really couldn't figure out exactly when I'd started liking Owen. But in a weird way, that made the idea of telling him seem a little easier. I wouldn't be changing our friendship, because it had been changing for a while.

"Thanks, Mom," I said. She ruffled my hair as she headed to the door.

"Anytime."

♪

Ridgewood's gym seemed brighter than normal, especially compared to Millican's gym at the dance last night. Mom and Dad helped me carry the display board and my notes inside, where we found a long line behind a booth with a sign that said REGISTRATION. Standing on my toes, I peered around the gym. Long rows of tables stretched all the way to the other wall, most of which were already covered in display boards.

I'd known from the beginning that the science fair was open to all the middle schools in the district, but somehow I hadn't thought about just how many projects that would mean. The gym was swarming with kids, teachers, and parents. Suddenly, I felt a little silly for being so sure Owen and I would win. Alien Park was awesome, but there were bound to be a lot of really good projects here.

When we reached the booth, a woman with a long dark braid and glasses smiled up at us. "Name and school?"

"Holly Mead, Millican," I replied, watching as she ran her finger down a list.

"Mead, Mead . . ." She stopped, grabbing a pencil and Post-It note. "Here we are! Auxiliary gym, row E, table seven." She scribbled it down, then glanced back at her list. "Your partner's already there," she added cheerfully, handing me the note. "Sounds like you guys have a pretty cool project. Good luck!"

I grinned. "Thanks!" Feeling slightly more confident, I followed my parents across the hall. The smaller gym felt even more crowded. I craned my neck around, trying to get a good look at as many projects as possible as we headed down row E. Most just looked okay, although I thought I saw an actual robot arm on one table, which was pretty awesome.

"Holly, over here!"

Owen's little stepsister, Megan, waved frantically from where she sat perched on table seven. Mrs. Grady had her hand on Megan's back, watching as her husband Steve adjusted a massive television on a stand next to the table. Owen was connecting cables from the television to a laptop on the table. He was wearing jeans and a *Cyborgs versus Ninjas* T-shirt, which made laughter bubble up in my throat for some reason.

When he looked up and smiled at me, I felt a mini explosion of happiness and nervousness in the pit of my stomach.

"Hi, Holly!"

"Hi!" I said, and I probably would've stood there

grinning at him for the rest of the afternoon if Megan hadn't tugged my sleeve.

"That's for the cartoon!" she exclaimed, pointing at the television.

"It's enormous," I said. "Where did you guys get it, anyway?"

"It's from the faculty room," Owen told me. "I was just going to use the laptop, but the teacher helping us said we could borrow it. I figured it'll look more impressive, right?"

"For sure." I took the display board from Dad, who went over to help Steve with the television. Megan scooted over as I set the board up on the table.

"Did you know Owen *made* the cartoon?" she asked, eyes wide and serious.

I grinned. "Yup."

"He can *make cartoons*, Holly," she said reverently. "He is, like . . . the awesomest brother *ever*."

That made me laugh. "I'll bet," I said. Owen smiled, his face a little pink.

We had everything set up and ready almost forty-five minutes before our presentation time. "Why don't you two go check out the other projects?" Mrs. Grady said. "We'll stay here and keep an eye on everything."

So Owen and I wandered around the gym, stopping to check out some of the cool projects. The robot arm was great, and the table right behind ours had a tub filled with homemade biodegradable plastic goo that was pretty neat. When we walked into the main gym, I spotted Julia in the registration line with her dad.

"Hey!" She waved us over. "Did you guys do your presentation already?"

"Not till two," I said. "When's your time?"

"Two thirty, I think." Julia set her display board down. "Natasha's was so early. She texted before I even woke up."

I laughed. "Is she still here?"

"No, I think she went home to take a nap," Julia replied. "I told her I'd let her know when they pick the finalists at four o'clock, just in case she has to come back." She grinned at us. "You guys are *so* going to be finalists."

"How many do they pick?" I asked.

"I think the packet said twenty," said Owen. "Then they present one more time, and the judges award first, second, and third places."

I made a face. "Yikes. There are, like, hundreds of projects here, and only twenty finalists?"

Julia started to say something, but the registration woman waved her forward.

"We'll come see your presentation!" I said, and she smiled.

"Okay, see you!"

We wandered up and down the rows for another fifteen minutes and found Trevor and Brent setting up Attack of the Carrot Clones. Mrs. Driscoll stopped at their table, sipping a to-go cup of coffee and consulting a sheet of paper.

"Morning!" she said cheerfully. "Let's see . . . carrot clones is at three o'clock, right?"

"Yep," said Trevor, unfolding their display board.

"Excellent." Mrs. Driscoll smiled at me and Owen. "And Alien Park is in about twenty minutes!"

My stomach fluttered. "Yes. Are you coming to watch?"

"Of course!"

That made me feel slightly better. Maybe I could pretend I was just presenting to Mrs. Driscoll again, instead of the judges.

When we got back to the auxiliary gym, I grabbed Owen's arm and pointed to a group of adults standing in front of one of the tables. "Those must be the judges," I said, and we hurried over to watch the presentation. Two girls stood in front of their display board, which said LITTLE SHOP OF HORRORS: CAN CARNIVOROUS PLANTS MAKE A MEAL OUT OF YOU? In the center of the table sat a fake, but very cool-looking, Venus flytrap.

"This is going to be awesome," I decided.

Owen nodded in agreement. "Obviously."

It ended up being the best presentation we'd seen all afternoon. The girls talked about their research and experiments with real carnivorous plants that ate bugs, and whether some types of plants might eat small animals—or even people. While one girl explained that the plants typically wouldn't be able to digest anything besides insects, the other girl casually stuck her arm in the "mouth" of the model Venus flytrap. When it snapped shut, everyone—including me—jumped. A few people even screamed, then started laughing when she pulled her arm out with a grin.

"I can't believe I fell for that," I said, shaking my head.

Owen snickered. "Me neither."

I swatted his arm as we headed back to our table. "Hey, it made you jump, too!"

"Yeah, but you never jump at stuff like that in scary movies."

"Exactly." I smiled, secretly pleased he'd noticed.

Back at our table, Megan was watching the Alien Park commercial. "For about the hundredth time," Mrs. Grady said wearily. Mom beamed at Owen.

"I can't believe you made this!" she exclaimed. "Holly told me it was amazing, but still—I'm so impressed!"

"Thanks," Owen said, ducking his head. I started checking my flash cards to make sure they were in order, mostly because I was pretty sure our moms had just exchanged "aren't they adorable" looks. I wondered if they'd noticed the cartoon aliens of me and Owen in the UFO slingshot.

I saw the judges appear at the end of our row and did a quick count. "Three tables till it's our turn," I told Owen. He was hunched over the laptop, setting the commercial to play from the beginning. "That probably gives us about ten minutes."

"Okay."

We spent a few minutes double-checking everything while our parents walked over to watch the presentations before us. I was going over my notes again, trying to memorize as much as possible so I could make eye contact with the judges. Most of my teachers were always telling everyone to look up during presentations. And I had to admit, watching someone just read off their flash cards could get pretty monotonous.

Megan tugged Owen's sleeve. "Can we watch that other cartoon you made?"

Owen looked distracted. "What other cartoon?" he asked, his eyes still on the screen.

"You know, the one you made with that girl who's always calling. With the penguins."

I kept my gaze firmly on my flash cards, doing my best to look unconcerned. Even peripherally, I could tell Owen was blinking like crazy.

"Oh, that," he said. "Sorry, Megan—the judges are almost here. Maybe later, okay?"

"Okay."

Owen straightened, and I saw *Coming Soon . . . Alien Park!* frozen on the television screen. "She was just talking about Ginny," he told me. "From the workshop."

"I know!" I said. "I remember—the extra project you were doing."

"Right." Owen sounded nervous. "We finished last week, so I played it for Megan. And she's not *always* calling. Ginny, I mean. Megan just exaggerates everything. We've only talked three times since San Antonio."

I adjusted the display board so that it was closer to the edge of the table. "It's okay!" My voice came out kind of squeaky. "I don't, um . . . I mean, you had to work on that cartoon. And you're friends. Right?"

"Sure, I guess. I just . . ." Owen stared intently down at the table, messy blond bangs falling over his eyes. "I didn't want you to think I *liked* her, or anything. Because I—I don't."

"Oh." Suddenly, I found the table just as fascinating. "Okay."

"Holly? Owen?"

We spun around, equally red-faced, to find the judges waiting expectantly. Behind them, Mrs. Driscoll stood next to my and Owen's parents. Megan was already staring at the television with a rapt expression.

One of the judges, a tall man with graying hair, smiled at us. "Are you ready?"

"Oh! Yes," I said quickly, moving aside so they could see our display board. Owen hurried over to the laptop, and I cleared my throat. "Our project is called Alien Park," I began, and for the next few minutes I forced myself to focus on the presentation. The commercial was a huge hit—several people gathered to watch, laughing at the UFO slingshot and applauding when it was over. I described all of our habitats in detail, pointing out the illustrations on the board, and Owen explained a few of the other exhibits. Just like Mrs. Driscoll recommended, we focused more on the scientific stuff, and less on the rides. When we finished, the judges were smiling. The tall judge raised his hand.

"Can we see the cartoon again?" he asked with a wink, and everyone laughed. Mrs. Driscoll was beaming.

"Sure!" I grinned as Owen started the commercial from the beginning.

Once the judges had moved on to the next presentation, Mom pulled me aside for a hug.

"That was *great*," she said, grinning.

"You really know your stuff," Dad added. "Future scientist, huh?"

"Maybe, if being in a symphony doesn't work out," I replied, and they laughed.

After congratulating us, Mrs. Driscoll headed off to see Trevor and Brent's presentation, and Owen's family went to have a late lunch. "I think I need coffee," Dad said, and Mom immediately agreed. After they left, Owen and I walked over to the main gym to see Julia's presentation.

"It went well, right?" I asked anxiously. "Did I mix up the Mercury habitat with the one about Europa? Because—"

"No, you didn't," Owen said, laughing. "I think we did really well."

We kept going over our presentation point by point

and wondering how good of a shot we had at being finalists. Although the prospect of actually winning the science fair wasn't the only thing that had my stomach buzzing with nervous anticipation.

Chapter Fifteen

*A*fter watching Attack of the Carrot Clones, Owen and I found Julia's table in time to see her presentation with Kim, her lab partner. I tried to pay attention, but in my head I kept replaying the conversation Owen and I were having before the judges showed up. *I didn't want you to think I liked her,* he'd said. Thinking about it made my face feel all warm again.

When Julia finished, the three of us went to the vending machines, then sat outside talking to pass the time until the finalists were announced. It should have been relaxing, but I felt antsy. I wanted to talk to Julia about what was happening with Owen. Or I just wanted to talk to Owen. But because they were both here, I couldn't talk to either of them about it at all.

After what seemed like forever, the list of finalists was posted in the gym. A crowd gathered around, and I hopped up and down, trying to see. Julia squirmed and pushed her way to the front. When she came back, she was beaming.

"You guys are on the list!" she said excitedly. "I so knew it."

"Really?" I cried. Owen's eyes were wide.

"Yup!" Julia pulled out her phone. "I've gotta text Natasha to tell her she doesn't have to come back. Oh, Holly," she added. "Want to spend the night at Natasha's tonight? She asked earlier and told me to ask you, too, but I flaked out."

"Sure!" I said, still bouncing up and down in excitement. "I'll ask my parents when they get back."

"Cool!" Julia gave me a quick hug. "Good luck, I really hope you guys win! You'd better go get ready."

Julia headed off to find her parents, and Owen and I hurried to the auxiliary gym. "We might actually get to do that NASA tour!" I said, not caring that I was practically yelling. "How freaking cool would that be?"

Owen looked just as excited. "Really cool. Actually," he added as we reached the table, "my mom said that either way, we could take a day trip to Houston over the summer. I don't think we could do this exact tour with the astronaut trainings and everything, but NASA has other kinds of tours."

I fumbled with my flash cards, putting them back in order. "Really? Oh, I hope you get to go even if we don't win."

"She said, um . . ." Brushing the hair out of his eyes,

Owen opened the laptop. "She said I could invite you. If you want."

I stared at him. "Are you kidding? I'd love to come! Seriously?"

Owen laughed, his cheeks flushed. "Yeah."

Mom and Dad walked in as we were finishing setting up, and Owen's family arrived a minute later, followed by Mrs. Driscoll.

"These two are the only seventh-graders from Millican chosen as finalists," she informed our parents.

"Really?" I exchanged an awed look with Owen as I stacked my note cards on the table.

Mrs. Driscoll nodded. "We had two more pairs chosen, both in eighth grade. I'm so proud of you both!"

She, along with our parents, stood there beaming proudly at us. Owen ducked his head to look at his laptop screen, but I could tell he was smiling.

The judges showed up, and the gray-haired man rubbed his hands together when he saw the television. This time, I saw his name tag: MR. GILL. "All right, the cartoon! I should've brought popcorn," he said, and I giggled.

This time, our parents, the judges, and Mrs. Driscoll weren't the only ones watching. At least a dozen other kids and parents crowded around our table—I recognized one of the boys with the robot-arm project laughing at the UFO slingshot in the commercial. I was halfway through describing the Mercury habitat before I realized my note cards were still sitting on the table. But instead of panicking, it made me feel more confident. At some point, I must have memorized the whole presentation.

After we finished and the judges moved on to the next table, Owen and I headed back over to the main gym with our parents, Megan, and Mrs. Driscoll. The registration table was cleared, and I could see a stack of certificates. Before long, the woman with the braid and glasses was calling all the finalists forward to line up. I stood next to Owen, making a conscious effort not to bounce up and down on my toes again. Having all forty of us up there made me realize how slim our chances of winning were. Mr. Gill stepped forward.

"First of all, let's have a round of applause for all of the finalists in the Fifteenth Annual Oak Point School District Science Fair!" He clapped along with everyone else. "I can tell you, we had a pretty hard time narrowing these down," he went on. "We're so impressed with the quality of the projects here today."

The woman with the braid handed him a certificate, and he cleared his throat.

"Third place, with a prize of two hundred dollars, is awarded to . . . Alien Park! By Holly Mead and Owen Reynolds from Millican Middle School."

My breath flew out in a *whoosh*. Beaming, I walked forward with Owen to take the paper and shake hands with the other judges. We studied the certificate while Mr. Gill continued talking.

"Third place!" Owen's eyes were shining. "Wow."

"I know." I couldn't stop smiling. "So what are we gonna do with two hundred dollars?"

He shook his head. "I have no idea."

We watched as the two boys with the robot arm were given the second-place certificate. "And now, the grand prize," Mr. Gill announced. "A private tour of the NASA Space Center in Houston. And the winner is . . ." He paused, clearly enjoying the dramatic effect. "Little Shop of Horrors! By Valerie Wenger and Sarita Bose from Forest Hill Middle School!"

"The Venus flytrap!" I exclaimed, clapping extra loudly as the two girls stepped forward with huge grins. "That's so cool. I'm glad they won."

As soon as Mr. Gill finished talking, Mom and Dad came over for hugs, and Mrs. Driscoll insisted on taking a few pictures of Owen and me with the certificate. After she left, we walked back to the other gym with Steve, while Mrs. Grady hurried Megan to the restroom. "Way too much juice at lunch!" Mrs. Grady exclaimed. I snickered, watching Megan do a funny, hopping dance down the hall.

When Dad and Steve started wheeling the television stand back to the faculty room, Mom turned to me. "I think I'll go pull the car up," she said. "We had to park pretty far away."

"Okay!" I waved as she walked off. Owen was shutting down his laptop, so I started to take down the display board and accidentally knocked my note cards all over the floor. "Whoops."

Kneeling, I gathered the cards up, reading a few as I did. I was actually going to miss working on this project. Then I remembered something that made me laugh.

"I was *failing* this class," I told Owen, grinning. "At the beginning of the year. Isn't that weird?"

He glanced over from his laptop. "Just the first quiz, though," he said, coming around the table to help me.

"Yeah, but . . ." I gestured to the flash cards in my hand. "I don't know. It's funny how it changed without me even realizing it."

"What do you mean?"

"Just that I hated science," I said, stacking the cards together. "And now it's my favorite subject. I mean, after band, obviously."

Owen smiled. "Really?"

"Yeah." We stood up, and I set the cards back on the table.

"It's my favorite class, too," Owen told me.

I laughed. "Well, yeah. I kind of figured that."

"No, I mean . . ." Owen hesitated. "It's my favorite class because you're in it."

And suddenly, I realized this was the moment I was supposed to tell him. *I like you!* Three words, dancing around in my head. But my brain just wouldn't make my mouth actually say it.

So instead, I kissed him.

Chapter Sixteen

A wave of warmth washed over me, like a head-to-toe blush. Stepping back, I opened my eyes—when had I even closed them?—and stared at my sandals.

That did not happen. I so did not just kiss Owen in the middle of the gym.

Except I had.

All of a sudden, my hands were sweaty and my heart was pounding way too loudly in my ears. Why*whywhy* did I do that? Did I freak him out? Probably. I'd certainly freaked myself out. He was probably setting a blinking record right now. I should check. Okay. Time for damage control.

Taking a deep breath, I looked up at Owen. He was just staring at me, eyes wide. Not a single blink.

Oh my God. I broke his eyelids.

"Um . . ." Panicking, I wiped my hands on my shorts and took another step back. My elbow bumped the display board, which wobbled precariously for a second before falling backward. It knocked into the board set up on the table behind ours, and they both toppled over, taking the tub of biodegradable plastic goo with them.

"Watch out!" A tall blond girl pulled her partner, a glasses-wearing round-faced boy crouched in front of their table, out of the way just in time. The container hit the ground with a loud *thump*, and they both leaped back as the yellowish goo splashed all over the floor.

I stood frozen, hands pressed to my mouth. My face was still hot, although for entirely different reasons. After a few seconds of mortified silence, I lowered my hands. "I'm *so* sorry," I started, and the girl laughed.

"Hey, better now than before the judges saw it!" she said cheerfully. "No worries, it was an accident."

Leaning forward, I looked at the floor and winced. The plastic was still pouring from the overturned tub, which the boy quickly uprighted. Both our display boards were ruined.

Gingerly, the boy pulled a flash card from the mess, grinning as a long strand of yellow goo clung to it. "Wicked."

I forced a laugh. My relief that they weren't upset didn't make this any less humiliating. I couldn't bring myself to look at Owen, but I was acutely aware of him still standing next to me. Walking around the tables, I looked up and down the aisle and spotted a teacher. "I'll go get something to clean this up," I told the girl, my voice shaking a little.

"Okay! Hey . . ." She caught up with me after a few steps, looking concerned. "Are you all right? It's really not a big deal, you know. It's not like we were gonna keep the slime."

This time I laughed for real. "Okay. And yeah, I'm fine. Thanks."

She smiled, and I hurried down the aisle, feeling very much *not* fine at all.

A few minutes later, I returned with a few teachers carrying a bunch of cleaning supplies from the custodian's closet. Owen was nowhere to be seen, which made me equal parts relieved and terrified. Did he actually leave?

Apparently, the blond girl had noticed me looking around. "He's just throwing the display boards away," she explained, grabbing a roll of paper towels.

"Oh, okay."

We had to scrape up most of the plastic stuff with dustpans before getting started with the mops. I was wiping off the table when Owen came back. I glanced at him just long enough to notice some of the yellow goo had gotten on his *Cyborgs* T-shirt. Stellar.

Dad and Steve showed up with Mrs. Grady and Megan, and they helped us finish cleaning up. Once the teachers left to return the supplies, I apologized to the blond girl and her partner again. I could sense Owen watching me.

Suddenly, I wanted nothing more than to not be in this gym anymore. Making an effort to sound as normal as possible, I turned to Dad and smiled. "Ready? Mom pulled the car up, she's probably wondering where we are."

We walked out with Owen's family, and I was relieved to see Mom's car right outside the entrance. "Bye!" I waved at Owen without actually looking at him, then slipped into the backseat and slammed the door closed.

Mom was beaming at me in the rearview mirror. "Third place! I can't get over it. Do you and Owen know what you want to do with the prize money?" Her brow furrowed, and she twisted around in her seat. "Holly, are you okay?"

"Yup!" Fake confidence. I had it down to an art form. "I don't know what we're going to do with it! I guess we'll talk about it Monday." *Among other things*, I added silently. My stomach started knotting up. "Hey, is it okay if I spend the night at Natasha's?"

Mom glanced at Dad. "I don't see why not," she said, and he nodded in agreement.

"Thanks!" Drumming my fingers on my knee, I stared out the window as our car joined the line leaving the parking lot.

I needed to talk to Julia and Natasha, stat.

𝄞

The knots in my stomach hadn't loosened one bit by the time I got to Natasha's house. Ringing the bell, I took a slow, deep breath and tried to relax. It didn't work.

Mrs. Prynne opened the front door, holding her purse. "Oh, Holly!" she smiled, standing back to let me in. "Thought you were the pizza guy. How's everything?"

"Good," I lied. "How are you?"

"Fine, thanks." She set her purse on a small table in the foyer. "The girls are upstairs—I'll let you know when the food's here."

"Thank you!" I said, even though just the thought of pizza made my stomach feel ten times worse. Clutching my overnight bag, I raced up the stairs and burst into Natasha's room.

Julia looked up from where she sat on the floor, painting Natasha's toes. "Hey!" she exclaimed. "So how'd it go?"

It took me a second to realize she meant the awards. "Oh, that," I said. "Good. We got third place."

Natasha's mouth fell open. "Whoa, really? That's awesome!"

"Nice!" Julia grinned. "That was what, two hundred dollars? Do you—" She stopped, squinting at me. "What's wrong? You look all . . . freaked out."

"I, um . . ." Sighing, I dropped my bag on the floor and braced myself. "I kissed Owen."

I'd spent the whole car ride over preparing myself for a lot of teasing. Instead . . . nothing. I thought I saw a flicker of excitement on Natasha's face, but Julia's expression didn't change at all. No one spoke for what felt like ages, until I couldn't take it anymore.

"Hello?" I cried. "Did you not hear me? I *kissed Owen*."

Julia nodded slowly. "But, I mean . . . just as friends, right?"

At that, Natasha started laughing so hard she fell to one side and knocked over the bottle of nail polish. Julia looked at me expectantly, although now I could tell she was trying not to laugh, too. Despite everything, I couldn't help but smile.

"Pretty sure it wasn't a 'just friends' thing." Kneeling, I uprighted the bottle. Frosty pink polish was spreading out over the paper towels they'd used to cover the rug. "Here's the funny part—and by funny, I mean completely and totally humiliating," I added, gesturing to the spilled nail polish. "This is kind of what happened right after I kissed him. Only, like, a hundred times messier."

Natasha sat up straight again. "What are you talking about?"

So I told them the whole story about the plastic goo. When I finished, Natasha's eyes were tearing up from trying not to laugh again. Julia patted my knee sympathetically.

"That's rough," she said. "But you talked to him after, right?"

"Hang on, hang on!" Natasha nudged my arm. "Forget the embarrassing part for a sec and rewind to the kissing."

I picked at a loose thread in the rug. "I just kind of did it without thinking. I wanted to tell him that . . . you know, that I like him, but . . ."

"Well, I'm pretty sure he knows now," Natasha said, giggling. "So?"

I blinked. "So?"

"So how was it?" She paused before adding: "Plastic goo spilling and all that aside." Julia snickered, and I smiled down at the rug, feeling my cheeks warm up again.

"It was . . . really, really nice," I admitted. After a few seconds, Julia grabbed a pillow and whacked me upside the head. "Hey!" I yelped. "What was that for?"

"You said you'd tell us if you liked Owen!" Julia said accusingly, although she looked more amused than mad. "I mean, we already knew because . . . well, duh. And we've been trying to lay off teasing you since spring break because I thought for sure you'd tell us when you were ready. Why didn't you say anything?"

"I'm sorry! I don't know." I grabbed a bottle of purple polish and unscrewed the top. "It took a while for me to figure it out, I guess. I didn't really decide I wanted to tell him until the dance last night." Making a face, I started applying a coat of polish to my thumbnail. "Now I've messed everything up."

Julia arched an eyebrow. "How? I mean, the goo thing was embarrassing and all, but it doesn't change the fact that you like each other. Oh . . ." Leaning against her bed, she gave me a knowing smile. "Let me guess. You took off without talking to him about it, right?"

I cringed. "Yeah. How'd you know?"

"Seth did the same thing," she said with a laugh.

"Remember when I asked him to the winter dance during PE? And he accidentally—"

"Almost broke your foot," Natasha interjected, snickering.

"Accidentally dropped a weight on my foot, which could happen to anyone," Julia went on, sticking her tongue out at Natasha. "He helped me get to the nurse's office, but then he took off. Because he was embarrassed." She gave me a pointed look. "But when I finally left, he was waiting out in the hall, and . . ." Shrugging, Julia grinned. "Well, it all turned out okay, right? We ended up laughing about it."

The knots in my stomach finally started to loosen. "So you think I can fix this?"

"Of course!" Natasha said. "Just talk to him."

"And tell him you're sorry for bailing," Julia added. "I'm sure he'll understand."

I nodded, feeling my shoulders relax. "Okay. Thanks, guys."

"Of course." Julia studied her pinky nail. "Hey, you don't mind if I tell Seth about you knocking over the plastic goo, right?" she asked, and I could hear the laughter in her voice. "It might make him feel better about dropping that w—"

The rest of her sentence was cut off by the pillow I'd launched at her head.

When I got home late Sunday afternoon, Chad was

leaving for work. Mom and I waved as he drove off.

"Has he re-trashed the Trash Mobile yet?" I asked, grabbing my overnight bag out of the backseat.

Mom laughed. "Actually, I peeked in yesterday afternoon and it looked pretty clean. Certainly cleaner than his bedroom," she added. "Any chance you want to tackle that?"

I made a gagging noise. "Not in a million years."

Upstairs, I flopped down on my bed with every intention of taking a nap. Julia and Natasha and I had stayed up way too late talking. Julia told us her dad was thinking of quitting his job to open a bakery, which her mom was nervous about but we all thought was awesome. Natasha told us she'd hung out with Gabe most of the morning at the science fair, and I had a feeling my hunch about them at the dance might be right. She also mentioned that he was thinking of running for student-council treasurer next year— apparently Ms. Gardner, her debate teacher, was already handing out election information packets. I made a joke about running for president, and we spent almost an hour coming up with silly campaign slogans. (Although in all honesty, I really was considering picking up one of those packets).

But my eyes were so grainy and scratchy, I couldn't fall asleep. Instead, I squinted at the Summer Countdown Calendar on my bulletin board. Only a week and a half till school was out. I remembered Owen inviting me to go to Houston and visit NASA over the summer, and found myself staring at the ghost-alligator drawing. Then I sat up. Sleep was definitely a lost cause.

After a minute, I decided to get out my horn. Chad wasn't home, so I could practice as much as I wanted without dealing with him kicking the wall. And tomorrow was our last chair test. Since it was also going to count as our audition for band next year, Mr. Dante had asked all of us, including the students in symphonic band and beginner band, to sign up for times to play before and after school for the next few days before the spring concert Thursday. I'd scheduled myself to play first thing tomorrow morning.

The étude didn't look all that difficult. But I'd practiced it a few times since Mr. Dante handed it out, and it was kind of . . . boring. Or at least, the way I played it was boring. Last semester, I'd had the same problem with a chorale for one of our chair tests. Mr. Dante had pointed out that even if I played it perfectly, that didn't mean I was making music out of it.

So I decided to forget about "perfect" and just have fun.

First, I played the whole étude as loud and fast as I could, which left me breathless and laughing. Then I played it like a slow funeral march, holding out all the notes way too long. I tried flipping the dynamics, playing quiet when it was marked loud, and vice versa. I played the first half of the étude as one long crescendo, getting louder and louder until I reached the middle, then starting to decrescendo until the last measure was so soft I was barely playing at all. I messed with the tempo, too, speeding up in some places, slowing down in others.

A lot of what I did sounded ridiculous. But the more I played, the more I discovered ways to make the étude a lot cooler. There were a few measures near the end with a busy rhythm that, when I sped up the tempo just a little, sounded really tense. And if I stretched out the high note at the end of the phrase, then played slightly softer in the next few measures, it was like all that tension just released.

I kept experimenting, looking for more little tricks like that, until the étude went from "perfect but boring" to something I'd actually want to listen to.

Chad came home with a bunch of Chinese food from Lotus Garden, which we ate with Mom and Dad while watching the first *House of the Wicked*. "Did you see the preview for that mutant-clown movie?" Chad asked me. "Looks kind of cool."

I nodded in agreement. "Yup, I really want to see it."

"I honestly don't know where you two got this horror obsession from," Mom muttered, holding a carton of fried shrimp in front of her eyes to block the television.

Back in my room, I considered practicing some more, even though my lips were still pretty tired. But auditions weren't the real reason I was nervous about tomorrow. I'd been trying to distract myself all day, but it was time to figure out what I was going to say to Owen.

It's my favorite class because you're in it. I felt kind of giddy every time I thought about him telling me that. Which was immediately followed by a dose of guilt when I remembered how I'd been in such a hurry to get out of there.

Glancing at the stack of Warlock cards on my dresser, I suddenly had an idea. I opened my desk, which was mostly filled with old notebooks and quizzes from last semester. Tucked away in the back was a different set of cards—the ones Owen had made to help me study for science at the beginning of the year.

I flipped through them, grinning at some of the pictures (the mouse wearing a wizard's hat was still my favorite). Then I dug out a pack of note cards and some colored pencils.

An hour later, I had ten of the most hilariously awful drawings ever. I tried the wizard mouse, along with a few cyborgs and ninjas, crazy Santas wielding band instruments, mutant clowns, alien fish, and, on the last card, both of our characters from *Prophets*, driving a tank that for some reason came out looking like a giant radio with wheels.

After scribbling a few words on the back of each card, I laid them out in order.

BET YOU

I CAN

GUESS THE

ENDING TO

MUTANT CLOWNS

FROM

PLANET Z!

WANT TO

MAKE IT

A DATE?

Smiling, I shuffled the cards so they were out of order, secured them with a rubber band, and stuck them in my backpack. I was definitely no artist, but hopefully Owen would like these all the same.

Chapter Seventeen

*M*om dropped me off at school Monday morning at what she called "an absurd hour." She kind of had a point—I'd never seen the halls so quiet. But I wanted to warm up before my audition.

When I walked into the cubby room and saw a sixth-grade boy already opening his French horn case, I was a little surprised.

"Hi!" I said. "Are you auditioning this morning, too?"

"Yes." He sounded nervous. "Are you?"

"Yup! I'm Holly," I added, setting my case down.

"I'm Brian."

On my way to the practice rooms, I checked the audition schedule on Mr. Dante's door. Natasha was right after me, then Brian. He was here extra early, too, I thought with a smile.

I warmed up slowly, then played through the étude. I could hear Brian playing in the room next door. He sounded great, especially for a beginner. On my way back to Mr. Dante's office, I paused outside Brian's door to listen a little longer, wondering if all the beginner horns were this good. No matter what, we'd have a pretty awesome French horn section next year in advanced band, which made me happy.

Mr. Dante's door was already open. Inside, he'd set up a chair and a music stand. "Morning, Holly!" he said, setting a to-go cup of coffee on his desk. "So you signed up for the very first spot—why am I not surprised?"

I grinned, setting my folder on the music stand. "I just met one of the beginner French horns. He sounds really good."

Glancing at the list on his door, Mr. Dante smiled. "Brian, yeah. He's quite the perfectionist. Reminds me of a certain seventh-grader at the beginning of this year, actually," he added pointedly, and I laughed. "Do you need to warm up, or are you ready?"

"I'm ready!" After moving the music stand a little closer, I sat up straight, lifted my horn, and played.

Just like yesterday, I focused on making the étude sound cool—a song I'd actually want to listen to. I added a few of the little touches I'd rehearsed, like pushing the tempo in certain places, or playing soft in measures with no dynamic markings. But there were a few spontaneous changes, too. One phrase in particular came out light and staccato, which surprised me—it almost sounded playful. When I finished, I set my horn in my lap and studied the sheet music, chewing my lip. I definitely hadn't played it exactly the way it was written . . . but I really, *really* liked how it had sounded.

It was a few seconds before I realized Mr. Dante was beaming.

"Now *that*," he said, "was musical."

Blushing, I smiled. "Thanks. It's okay that I kind of, um . . . changed it a little?"

"You didn't change it," Mr. Dante told me. "You *interpreted* it. You took the notes on the page, and you played them the way *you* hear the music. Big difference, right?"

"Yeah." I nodded, pleased. "It's a lot more fun this way."

"I agree," Mr. Dante said, scribbling something down in his notebook. "Well, if you've made this much progress in seventh grade, I can't wait to see what next year's going to be like."

I grinned. "Thanks! Me too."

Natasha was waiting outside the office when I opened the door, her eyes wide. "Holly, you sounded *amazing!*" she said. "Seriously . . . wow."

"Thank you!" I stepped out of the way. "Good luck!"

"Wait for me, okay?" Natasha asked as she walked into the office. "We can walk to the cafeteria together—I think they've got pancakes for breakfast."

"Okay!"

I noticed Brian perched on the edge of a chair, wearing an anxious expression. "You sounded great in the practice room," I told him with an encouraging smile.

"Oh . . . thank you," he said, looking surprised.

"Good luck!" I headed back to the cubby room, feeling ridiculously cheerful. After putting my horn away, I took the cards I'd made for Owen out of my backpack. I checked to make sure they were shuffled before looking in Owen's cubby, which was empty except for his music folder. So he'd have to come to the band hall before first period to put his horn up, I realized. I shoved the cards to the back of the cubby. Then I thought he might not find them back there, so I pulled them to the very front. Then I started worrying someone else would see them, so maybe I should—

"Holly?"

I spun around, still holding the cards. Owen stood right behind me, obviously confused. Well, at least his eyelids were working again.

"Owen, hi! I didn't, um . . ." I stopped, clearing my throat to get rid of the helium-balloon pitch. "You're here early! Is your audition this morning?"

He shook his head. "It's after school. But I've got a group presentation in Spanish first period, and we're supposed to meet in five minutes." I saw him glance curiously at the cards in my hand, and realized I was still standing in front of his cubby.

"Oh sorry!" I stepped aside quickly, waiting until he put his case away before holding the cards out. "These are for you."

Owen stared at the top card, which just said GUESS THE. After a second, he looked up. "Is this for class or something?"

"No, it's . . ." I couldn't seem to get my voice back to normal. "It's a game. Just for you, though—don't try to play it with anyone else!" I added quickly, and the blinking started again.

"A game?"

I nodded. "Kind of . . . well, you'll see." I took a deep breath. "And I know you're in a hurry, but I'm really sorry I left so fast at the science fair after, um . . ." I felt my face start to heat up. "After, you know, we cleaned up all that plastic stuff. I just—I guess I was sort of embarrassed about knocking it over, and—"

"I'm starving," Natasha announced as she entered the cubby room, startling me. She started to say something else before she noticed me and Owen standing there, both pink-faced. Looking amused, Natasha quickly opened her case and placed her horn inside. "Meet you later in the cafeteria?" she asked me lightly.

"Actually, I've really got to get to Spanish," Owen said. "But I'll, um . . ." He glanced at the cards before giving me a quick, shy smile. "I'll see you in fourth, I guess?"

I smiled back, relieved. "Okay, yeah."

After he left, I let out a long, slow breath. "Ugh."

"I'm *so* sorry!" Natasha said, giggling. "I had no idea he was in here. So what happened?"

I wrinkled my nose. "Well, I apologized. But that was it."

"What was he holding—did you give him something?"

"Yeah. I kind of made a card game." I picked up my backpack. "Let's go get breakfast, okay? You're going to make fun of me for this, so I at least deserve some pancakes first."

𝄞

"Hang on—you asked him out with flash cards?" Eyebrows arched, Gabby snuck a handful of M&M's into her mouth as Mr. Franks moved around the room, handing back our research papers.

"It sounds dorky when you say it like that," I said.

She snickered. "Um, maybe because it *is* dorky. However . . ." Gabby paused to shove the M&M's into her pencil bag as Mr. Franks stopped next to her, stepping around the poster boards leaning against the side of her desk.

"Are these for another class?" he asked, nudging the poster boards.

Gabby nodded. "History," she mumbled around a mouthful of chocolate.

"Ah." Mr. Franks set her paper down with a bemused smile. "Let's keep the candy put away for the rest of class, shall we?"

"Yes, sir," Gabby replied with a salute. Mr. Franks handed me my paper, then continued down the row.

I flipped open the cover page and sighed in relief—92. After all that research and revising, it was nice to get an A. I almost felt like I knew Eleanor Roosevelt better than I knew myself.

"Anyway, I know Owen will like the cards," I told Gabby, sticking my paper in my binder. "Dorky or not."

"I never said he wouldn't," she replied, grinning. "Actually, I was going to say that I bet he loves it. Further proof you're perfect for each other, I guess."

I felt pretty giddy for most of the morning. But by the time the bell rang to end third period, it was more like half giddy, half nervous. I *did* think Owen would like the cards, but there was still the matter of actually talking to him about going from being friends to . . . whatever we were now.

Pushing the band-hall doors open, I spotted Owen right away, already in his chair and talking to Trevor. I hurried into the cubby room, feeling weirdly shy all of a sudden. When I pulled my horn case out of my cubby, a sheet of paper fluttered to the ground. My heart thumped extra hard when I realized it was a sketch.

I picked it up, facing my cubby so no one could see the enormous smile stretching my cheeks. It was the cartoon aliens from our commercial—the green ones, a boy with yellow hair and a girl with a brown ponytail, holding hands. They were in the UFO slingshot, which was under attack by some pretty wicked-looking mutant clowns. In the background, along with a bunch of stars, I saw a small planet labeled Z.

Even though Owen probably hadn't had much time between classes to work on it, I was amazed at how good the sketch was anyway. It was definitely going up on my bulletin board next to Holly's Haunted Zoo.

Turning, I saw Julia across the cubby room, putting her clarinet together and talking to Natasha. Next to her, Gabby was struggling to keep the poster boards rolled up as she stuck them in her cubby. I practically skipped over to them.

"Look!" I held out the sketch, then lowered it when Julia and Natasha shrieked. "What?"

"Those clowns are even worse than the ones on that movie poster!" Julia cried, still shielding her eyes. "Why would you show me that?"

"No, it's . . ." I stopped, laughing. "I'm sorry! I forgot about the clowns. But look at the other part!"

Cramming the last poster board away, Gabby took the sketch. "Oh my God, is that alien Holly and alien Owen?" When I nodded, she cracked up. "I was so right—you guys are a match made in heaven. Or in space, I guess," she added, handing the sketch back. I slipped it behind the sheet music in my folder, still smiling uncontrollably.

We walked into the band hall just as Mr. Dante stepped onto the podium. "Everyone take your seats, please."

Feeling self-conscious again, I sat down in my chair and smiled at Owen. But before I could say anything, even just a whispered "thanks," Gabby reached behind

Natasha and me and thumped him on the back.

"Nice," she said with a wink before sitting down. Owen laughed a little, staring at his knees.

Mr. Dante started our warm-ups, and I did my best to focus. Concentration was pretty much a lost cause, though. I kept glancing at the clock and trying to figure out what to say after rehearsal. Because I was determined to talk to Owen before lunch.

Apparently he had the same idea, because he took an extra-long time putting his music away when Mr. Dante dismissed us. I dawdled, too, cleaning my mouthpiece about a dozen times. Julia and Natasha put their instruments up and hurried out of the band hall without waiting for me, like they'd read my mind.

Owen and I walked to the cubby room together. Gabby was pulling the rolled-up poster boards from her slot. Just a few others were left, including Trevor. Who, I realized, was probably expecting to walk to lunch with us, since we all sat together.

But to my surprise, he walked over to Gabby. "History presentation?" Trevor asked, pointing to the poster boards.

"Yeah, but not till sixth," Gabby said. "I've been hauling this stuff around all day—I didn't have time to drop it off in the morning, and . . ." She stopped, staring as Trevor took two of the poster boards. "Uh, what are you doing?"

Trevor shrugged. "You've got PE next, right? I've got lunch, so I can help you take this stuff to the gym first."

When Gabby continued to gape at him, he rolled his eyes and headed out of the cubby room. "You could try saying thank you, Princess Flores!" he called over his shoulder.

After a second, Gabby grabbed her backpack and hurried after him. I heard her say "Thank you, Mr. Chivalrous!" in a singsong voice just before the band-hall doors swung closed behind them.

Owen and I stared at each other. "What just happened?" I said in disbelief. Owen shook his head, laughing.

"No idea."

An awkward silence descended, and I stared at my shoes. Then Owen cleared his throat.

"Thanks for the cards." I looked up to find him smiling. "Those pictures were, um . . ."

"Awful?" I supplied. "The worst drawings ever?"

"I recognized most of them, but . . ." Pulling the cards out of his pocket, Owen flipped through them and held one out. "What *is* that, exactly?"

I tried to keep a straight face. "What do you think it is?"

Dutifully, Owen studied the card again, pressing his lips together like he was trying not to laugh. "Well, it looks like a rock with eyes wearing a party hat. And . . . is that a worm?"

I sighed. "That's the tail. It's a mouse in a wizard's hat. From the study cards you made for science last semester, remember?"

Owen blinked. "Oh yeah. Wait—do you still have those?"

"Of course!"

The way he smiled when I said that made me blush. I hadn't thought saving those cards was a big deal, but apparently it was.

"So, that sketch . . ." I swallowed nervously. "That was a yes? About the, um . . . the date?" Owen nodded, and I exhaled, beaming. "Do you maybe want to have dinner at my house sometime, too?" I asked. "My mom said I could invite you. And don't worry, my parents won't let Chad be all annoying like when he drove us to the movies. He just likes to do the whole boyfriend-interrogation thing. I mean, not that you're my boyfriend. Unless you want to be? I mean, do you . . ." I trailed off. This was a pretty epic ramble, even for me.

Owen was still smiling. "Yes."

"Okay," I said. "Wait—yes to which question?"

He laughed, blushing. "Um . . . all of them."

"Oh."

I stood there for a second, feeling light-headed and wondering if I had the courage to kiss him again. But as it turned out, it didn't matter. Because this time, he kissed me first.

Chapter
Eighteen

*F*ive final exams, four and a half days, and one concert to go until summer. It felt like time sped up the closer I got to the end of my Summer Countdown Calendar. I'd been going to Owen's house almost every day after school—in between studying for our final exams, we were working on a new, secret cartoon project for the spring concert.

On Wednesday night, Owen came over to my house for dinner. We ordered a bunch of food from Lotus Garden, and (with the help of a few warning looks from Mom) Chad even managed to behave himself. Except for when I cracked open my fortune cookie and found a message that said LOVE IS ON THE WAY and he snorted Coke out his nose. (He wasn't so amused when his fortune read YOU NEVER KNOW WHAT TREASURES YOU POSSESS . . . UNTIL YOU CLEAN YOUR ROOM. Judging from the look on Mom's face, I was pretty sure she'd snuck that one in there herself.)

When I walked into the band hall Thursday afternoon, I knew right away Mr. Dante had posted the final chair test results thanks to the small crowd around his office door. Standing on my toes, I saw two sheets: one with our chair order for the concert tonight, and one for next year's advanced band. When I found my name on the first sheet, my heart skipped a beat.

French Horn

1. *Holly Mead*
2. *Natasha Prynne*
3. *Owen Reynolds*
4. *Brooke Dennis*

The French horn section for next year's band was the same, but with the name Brian Parry in place of Brooke's. The sixth-grade boy, I remembered with a grin—he'd managed to beat the few seventh-graders in symphonic band. *He must be excited.* I sure had been when I'd made advanced band as a seventh-grader.

And now I was first chair! The only other time this year I'd been first chair was after I was ranked higher than Natasha at all-region auditions. And I'd always wondered if that had been some sort of fluke, since Mr. Dante had never placed me higher than Natasha. But now he had.

When I saw Natasha walk into the band hall, I couldn't help feeling a tiny bit apprehensive. I watched as she came over to check the results. Her face lit up, and she looked around till she spotted me.

"I *knew* it!" Natasha hurried over and gave me a

quick hug. "Seriously, I so knew you'd be first chair after I heard your audition." Relief flooded me, because she seemed genuinely excited.

"Just for now," I said, grinning. "We'll have lots of chair tests next year, right?"

Natasha nodded. "Yup. You'd better watch out," she teased as we headed to the cubby room.

𝄞

"Hopefully this is the last time we have to wear these." Julia made a face, poking at the velvet bow on the puffy sleeve of her dress.

I nodded. "Yeah. Maybe we can do a bake sale in the fall again."

We headed back to the band hall for warm-ups, passing Aaron and Liam on the way. It suddenly dawned on me that this was our last performance ever with all the eighth-graders. The thought made me a little sad.

Although next year I'd be an eighth-grader, which was pretty awesome (and maybe a tiny bit intimidating).

After warm-ups, we headed to the auditorium to watch the beginner band's performance. I sat between Owen and Natasha. As soon as I spotted Brian up on the stage, I pointed him out.

"He's in our section next year," I told them. "He's *really* good. And Mr. Dante said he's a perfectionist, like . . ." I stopped, and Owen laughed.

"Like you?"

"Well . . . yeah," I admitted.

Natasha nodded approvingly. "Excellent."

We left before the symphonic band's last song to get our instruments and line up outside of the backstage entrance. Before I knew it, we were filing onstage and taking our seats. Seeing the auditorium filled with people made me smile. UIL had been fun, but performing in front of an actual crowd was always way better.

Mrs. Park talked for a few minutes before we played, and the band boosters presented little gift bags to all the eighth-graders. I noticed the laptop and projector set up to the side of the stage, and smiled to myself. Mrs. Park was the only one who knew about the surprise Owen and I had planned for Mr. Dante.

We played a few fun, easy songs Mr. Dante had given us after UIL first. Then it was time for one last performance of "Labyrinthine Dances," which was the part I was most excited about. I'd triple-checked to make sure my dad had brought his video camera before we'd left the house.

And it was a good thing, too. By now, we all practically had the song memorized. The applause when we finished seemed to go on much longer than usual. It took a few seconds for me to realize Mrs. Park had flipped on the projector.

"Before the last song, a few of our students have a little surprise for Mr. Dante," she said cheerfully. "Do either of you want to say anything?" she added, looking from me to Owen.

Red-faced, Owen just shook his head. I grinned at Mrs. Park. "Just play it!" I called, and she smiled.

"Here we go!" She tapped PLAY, and we all shifted in our seats to see the giant projector screen. When the title *Evil Robot Band Directors* appeared, everyone started to laugh, including Mr. Dante.

Our cartoon was only half a minute long, but I had to admit it was pretty hilarious. A bunch of crazed robots waving conductor's batons crashed a rehearsal and started wrecking the band hall, until the superhero band director (who kind of looked like a cross between Mr. Dante and Superman) flew in and used his powers to turn them all into trophies. When it finished, I saw Mr. Dante take off his glasses to wipe his eyes, his shoulders shaking with laughter.

It took a minute after the cartoon ended for all the giggling to die down so we could play the last song. And no sooner had we played the last note than Gabby started cackling again. "I'm so getting Dante a cape for concerts next year," she said as we filed off the stage.

Out in the lobby, I spotted my parents leaving the auditorium. Chad came out a few seconds later, along with Amy.

"That's . . . weird," Trevor said, and I glanced at him.

"You didn't know they were dating?"

"No, I found out a few weeks ago," Trevor replied. "It's still weird, though."

"You're telling me." I squinted at Chad. "God, I think my brother actually used *gel* in his hair."

After saying hello to Owen's family, I left him with Megan begging to see the robot cartoon again and walked over to my parents. Dad was standing with his hands behind his back, and they were both smiling in a weird way, like they had a secret.

"Fantastic job!" Mom exclaimed, giving me a hug. "The music *and* the cartoon—that was too funny!"

"Thanks!" I said. "Did you record everything?"

Dad nodded. "Yes, ma'am. And . . ." He and Mom exchanged grins, and I narrowed my eyes.

"What's going on?"

"Well, we've been talking lately about how well you've done in band this year," Mom said. "First chair, all-region . . . so we have a little surprise for you."

Dad held out a piece of paper. I took it, read the first line, and almost dropped my horn.

DEAR CAMPER,

WE ARE HAPPY TO CONFIRM YOUR REGISTRATION FOR LAKE LINDON BAND CAMP!

"Are you *serious!*" I cried, hopping up and down. "Really, I can go?"

"Really," Mom said, beaming. "They sent a whole packet—it's at home. There's a packing list, a schedule, I think even a few exercises for you to start practicing." She laughed at the expression on my face. "I have to admit, this camp looks kind of like Holly Heaven."

"Thank you!" I yelled, hugging them both. "Can I go tell Julia and Natasha?"

Dad nodded. "Go ahead. I think we should go say

hello to Amy's parents, don't you?" he added, smiling at Mom.

"Absolutely," she said, her voice serious. "I'm sure Chad will appreciate it."

I couldn't stop smiling as I hurried across the lobby to where Natasha stood talking with Julia and her parents. This summer was going to be *awesome*.

Chapter Nineteen

After two days of final exams, everyone was pretty wired Wednesday morning. And since it was both a half day and the last day of school, most teachers seemed to pretty much give up on doing any sort of real lesson. In English, Mr. Franks had us play a trivia game about Shakespeare, which led to Gabby doing an overly dramatic reading of Romeo's speech to Juliet that gave everyone a serious case of the giggles. During PE third period, Coach Hoffman sipped what I bet was not her first cup of coffee while watching us play a rather rowdy game of volleyball.

Since school would be dismissed after fourth period, Mr. Dante put us to work cleaning the band hall. We stacked chairs and music stands, cleaned out our cubbies, and covered all the instruments in the percussion section. Then we spent the rest of the class signing yearbooks. The chatter grew steadily louder and more animated, with someone glancing up at the clock every few seconds.

I joined Aaron and Liam for a few minutes, swapping yearbooks and listening with interest as they talked about the camp they'd be doing at Ridgewood for marching band later this summer. "It's going to be weird next year without you guys," I told them, writing a few funny tips in Aaron's yearbook about how to keep his music folder organized.

Aaron nodded. "But hey, the year after that you'll be in marching band with us."

"That's true!" I said, although that seemed like an awfully long time from now. Brooke sat down with us, taking my yearbook from Aaron and handing hers to Liam. As soon as they started talking about camp again, she leaned closer to me.

"So Ms. Gardner told me you picked up one of those election packets!" she said, smiling. "Are you running for student council next year?"

I blushed. "Um, I'm not sure yet. It looks really fun, though."

"It is." Brooke tapped her pen on her knee. "What position are you thinking about?"

"Well . . ."

She laughed. "President, huh?"

"Maybe, yeah," I admitted.

"Awesome!" Beaming, Brooke started scribbling in my yearbook. "We'll start a new French horn–section tradition." She moved her hand, and I grinned when I saw what she'd written: HOLLY FOR PRESIDENT!

I had to admit, that looked pretty cool.

After promising her, Aaron, and Liam that I'd be at the first Ridgewood football game to see the half-time show, I headed to the front of the room and sat cross-legged next to Owen. He was drawing what was probably his tenth "Superhero Dante destroying robots" sketch in a yearbook—apparently, it was a pretty popular request.

I flipped through my own yearbook to read some of the notes, giggling when I noticed the word BEES! in giant letters, with Trevor's tiny signature beneath it. Next to that, Gabby had added a funny sonnet about bees and candy—apparently, our Shakespeare trivia game in English had put her in a poetic mood. Julia and I had kept our tradition of writing each other ridiculous, lengthy notes in a huge spiral that took up most of a page. And Natasha had written a bunch of cheesy quotes from her favorite romance movies under her note to me, probably because I'd done the same thing in her yearbook, only with horror quotes.

Natasha finished signing Owen's yearbook and handed it to me. "Julia has an idea," she announced. "And you have to say yes."

"Yes," I joked, giving Owen my yearbook. I smiled when he flipped to a blank page in the back and started sketching.

Julia sat up straight and gave me a stern look. "First," she said, ticking the points off on her fingers. "Natasha's going to read that book I lent you. The scary one."

"Really?" I glanced at Natasha, who nodded.

"Second . . ." Julia took a deep breath and closed her eyes. "I'll do one—*one*—roller coaster with you guys this summer."

"And we get to pick which one," Natasha told me with a grin. My eyes widened.

"Wow! That's—hang on." I crossed my arms, looking suspiciously at them. "I'm guessing I have to do something, too?"

Julia smiled. "Yup. But yours is easy."

"Super simple," Natasha agreed. "All you have to do is come see the sequel to *Seven Dates* with us this summer."

"Ugh, they made a *sequel* to that?" I cried as Owen let out a snort of laughter. "No. No way."

"Come on, Holly!" Julia poked my arm. "You guys love roller coasters, so I'll give them another shot. Natasha's reading that book you and I like, even though it's pretty creepy. So you can give romance movies another try, because we love them. Okay?"

"Okay, okay." Groaning, I squeezed my eyes closed. "So what's it called? No, let me guess . . . *Seven Break-Ups*. Or maybe *Eight Dates*. *Seven Weddings*? Or—"

"It's called," Julia interrupted in a haughty tone, "*The Eighth Date*."

Owen ducked his head, still laughing, while I rolled my eyes. "Oh my God, seriously?"

Natasha smiled sweetly. "Seriously. So you'll go with us, right?"

"Yeah." Sighing, I glanced at Owen. "Want to come?"

He stopped laughing, eyes wide. "Nooooo . . . ," he said without looking up from his sketch, which made Julia and Natasha giggle.

I opened Owen's yearbook while they continued talking about the movie. I kept trying to sneak glances at what Owen was drawing—it was hard to see with his arm in the way, but it took up the whole page. I found a blank space in the back of his yearbook and pulled my knees into my chest so no one could read as I wrote. It wasn't sappy or anything, mostly a bunch of inside jokes about *Prophets* and *Cyborgs* and science class . . . although I did add a giant heart next to my signature. I mean, it was pretty much the only thing I could draw that was actually recognizable.

"One minute left, you guys!" Julia exclaimed suddenly, pointing to the clock. Natasha let out a little cheer as she leaned over to get her yearbook from Sophie.

I set Owen's yearbook next to him, watching his pen fly over the page. After a second, he glanced up and sighed. "I don't think I'm going to finish before the bell."

"That's okay." I leaned over to see what he'd drawn so far, but he snapped my yearbook closed.

"It's a work in progress," he told me, smiling. "Do you mind if I take it home?"

"Sure!" I said. "When can I get it back?"

"How about tomorrow? Thursday's still *Prophets* day, right?" Owen's eyes widened. "Hey, maybe the expansion pack will come in by then!" We'd used our science fair prize money to order it over the weekend. It made sense—after all, *Prophets* had been the whole inspiration behind our Alien Park project to begin with.

I grinned. "It's a date."

Picking up my backpack, I took Owen's hand. After telling Mr. Dante to have a good summer, we joined Julia, Natasha, and the rest of the band at the door. Gabby started counting down the seconds until the bell, and soon everyone was shouting along with her, our voices getting louder and louder. Even though I was excited about summer vacation, I couldn't help feeling a little sad that this year was over.

But, I told myself with a smile, next year would be even better.

About the Author

Michelle Schusterman is a former band director and forever band geek, starting back in the sixth grade when she first picked up a pair of drumsticks. Now she writes books, screenplays, and music in New York City, where she lives with her husband (and bandmate) and their chocolate Lab (who is more of a vocalist).

INDEX

American Plantations Token.................. 16
Anthony, Susan B., Dollars 122
Auctori Connec Coppers (Connecticut) 27-29
Auctori Plebis Token 34

Baldwin & Co. (Private Gold) 180
Baltimore, Lord (Maryland)................... 15
Bar Cent.................................... 34
Barber Dimes 1892-1916...................... 80
Barber Quarter Dollars 1892-1916............. 92
Barber Half Dollars 1892-1915 106
Barry, Standish, Threepence (Baltimore, Md.)... 35
Bechtlers, The, Christopher and August 171-173
Bermuda (Sommer Islands).................... 13
Bicentennial Coinage................... 98, 112, 121
Bishop, Samuel (Connecticut) 27
Brasher, Ephraim, Doubloon................. 29
Brenner, Victor D. (Designer of Lincoln Cent)... 57
Britannia (1787 Coppers) 33
Buffalo Nickels (Indian Head) 1913-1938........ 66
Bullion Charts -
  Silver.................................. 188
  Gold 188
Bullion Coinage............................. 169

California Fractional Gold.................... 187
Carolina Elephant Tokens 19
Carolina Gold (Bechtler).................. 171-173
Cent, 1864, L on Ribbon 55
Cents, Large 1793-1857 46-53
Cents, Flying Eagle 1856-1858.............. 54
Cents, Indian Head 1859-1909............... 54-56
Cents, Lincoln 57-62
Cents, Steel 1943........................... 59
Chalmers, J., Silver Tokens (Annapolis, Md.).... 22
Charlotte, No. Carolina Branch Mint 7
Cincinnati Mining & Trading Co. (Private Gold) 178
Civil War Tokens 187
Clad Coinage 6, 85, 97, 111, 121
Clark, Gruber & Co. (Private Gold)........... 185
Cleaning of Coins........................... 11
Clinton, George, Copper (New York) 30
Colorado Gold Pieces........................ 185
Commemorative Coins, General Information ... 150
Commemorative Gold 166-168
Commemorative Silver...................... 150-166
Condition of Coins 10
Confederatio Coppers 25
Connecticut Coppers (Auctori Connec)........ 27-29
Continental Dollar, 1776..................... 23
Conway, J.J. & Co. (Private Gold)............. 186
Cox, Albion (New Jersey)..................... 31

Dahlonega, Ga., Branch Mint 7
Dimes....................................... 75-86
Dimes, Liberty Seated 1837-1891............. 77-80
Dimes, Barber 1892-1916 80-82
Dimes, "Mercury" Head 82-84
Dimes, Roosevelt 84-86
Distinguishing Marks 7-9
Dollar, Origin of 112
Dollars, Patterns (Gobrecht) 1836-1839........ 114
Dollars, Silver, Liberty Seated 1840-1873 115
Dollars, Trade 116-117
Dollars, Silver, Morgan Type 1878-1921........ 117
Dollars, Silver, Peace Type 1921-1935......... 120
Dollars, Eisenhower Type 1971-1978........... 121
Dollars, Susan B. Anthony Type 122
Dollars, Gold 1849-1889..................... 123
Dollars, Gold (California) 187
Double Eagles 1849-1933................... 144-150

Dubosq & Co. (Private Gold)................. 180
Dunbar & Co. (Private Gold)................. 181

Eagles 1795-1933........................... 138-144
Eisenhower Dollars 1971-1978............... 121
Elephant Tokens........................... 18, 19
Excelsior Coppers (New York) 30

Five Cent, Nickel 64
Five Cent, Silver........................... 69
Five Cent, Shield Type 1866-1883 64
Five Cent, Liberty Head 1883-1913............ 65
Five Cent, Indian or Buffalo Type 1913-1938 66
Five Cent, Jefferson Type 69
Flying Eagle Cent 1858, LG. and SM. Letters ... 54
Fifty Dollar Gold (Private)174, 175, 177, 179, 182, 183
Five Dollar Gold Pieces 131
Four Dollar Gold Pieces 131
Franklin, Benjamin - Fugio Cents 40
Franklin Press Token 35
French Colonies............................ 22
Fugio Cents 5, 40

George III - Immune Columbia................ 24
George III - Indian (New York) 30
George III - Vermont........................ 33
Georgia Gold (Reid)..................... 170, 171
Georgia Gold (Bechtler) 171
Gloucester Token 20
Goadsby, Thomas (New Jersey) 31
Gobrecht, Christian 114
Gold, Dollars 1849-1889..................... 123
Gold, $2.50 125
Gold, Three Dollars 130
Gold, Stella, $4.00 Patterns 131
Gold, Five Dollars......................... 131
Gold, Ten Dollars 138
Gold, Twenty Dollars....................... 144
Gold, Private or Territorial 170
Goodrich, John (Connecticut) 27
Granby Coppers (John Higley) 20

Half Cents................................. 42-45
Half Dime (LIBEKTY Variety 1800)........... 72
Half Dimes................................ 71-74
Half Dimes, Liberty Seated................. 73-74
Half Dollars 98-112
Half Dollars, Liberty Seated 102-106
Half Dollars, Barber 106-108
Half Dollars, Liberty Walking 108-109
Half Dollars, Franklin..................... 110-111
Half Dollars, Kennedy..................... 111-112
Half Dollars, Gold......................... 187
Half Eagles 1795-1929 131-138
Harmon, Rueben Jr. 32
Hibernia - Voce Populi Token................ 21
Hibernia Coins, William Wood 17, 18
Higley, John, Coppers (Granby, Connecticut).... 20
Hillhouse, James (Connecticut)............... 27
"Hogge Money" (Sommer Islands)............. 13
Hopkins, Joseph (Connecticut) 27
Hull, John (Mass. Colonial Silver).......... 13
Humbert, Augustus (U.S. Assayer) 174

Immune Columbia 24
Immunis Columbia......................... 24, 25
Indian - George III (New York) 30
Ingots, California Gold 174, 179

Jefferson, Thomas, Nickels 69
Jenks, Joseph 13

LIMITED EDITION, BLUE BOOK MEDALLION

In recognition of the 46th Annual edition of Whitman's *Handbook of United States Coins* ("Blue Book"), Whitman is offering a limited edition, proof-like, one ounce silver medallion. This one ounce of .999 pure silver was exclusively designed and struck for Whitman.

It is complimentary to and forms a beautiful collector's set with the special *A Guide Book of United States Coins* ("Red Book") medallion. Both of these outstanding medallions are excellent gifts and fine keepsakes.

Order your limited edition Blue Book medallion now while supplies last.

To order, fill in and mail the order blank below with check or money order for $10.95 (plus sales tax where applicable) plus the proof of purchase label from the front cover of this book. (Only one medallion may be ordered per proof of purchase.)

I understand I may return the medallion within 14 days and receive a full refund if not completely satisfied.

To order the Whitman Coin Dealer Directory, enclose an additional $1.50 along with your medallion order.

Mail To:
Whitman Coin Department
Western Publishing Company, Inc.
P.O. Box 700, M.S. #438
Racine, WI 53401

```
Place Proof of
Purchase Label Here
```

NAME _____
                    Please Print

ADDRESS _____

CITY _____ STATE _____ ZIP _____

PLACE OF PURCHASE _____

cut along line